Under the Wire

JULIE WHITE

sononis
PRESS
WINLAW, BRITISH COLUMBIA

Library and Archives Canada Cataloguing in Publication
White, Julie, 1958-
      Under the wire / Julie White.
ISBN 978-1-55039-198-5
      I. Title.
PS8645.H54U53 2012   jC813'.6   C2012-901959-3

Sono Nis Press most gratefully acknowledges support for our publishing
program provided by the Government of Canada through the Canada
Book Fund and the Canada Council for the Arts, and by the Province of
British Columbia through the British Columbia Arts Council and the
Book Publishing Tax Credit, Ministry of Provincial Revenue.

Edited by Laura Peetoom
Copy edited by Dawn Loewen
Proofread by Audrey McClellan

Published by
Sono Nis Press
Box 160
Winlaw, BC V0G 2J0
1-800-370-5228

Distributed in the U.S. by
Orca Book Publishers
Box 468
Custer, WA 98240-0468
1-800-210-5277

books@sononis.com
www.sononis.com

Printed and bound in Canada by Houghton Boston Printing.

Printed on acid-free paper that is forest friendly
(100% post-consumer recycled paper)
and has been processed chlorine free.

The Canada Council | Le Conseil des Arts
for the Arts | du Canada

*For pony horses everywhere,
and most especially to Keno, "The Spotted Wonder."
Thank you for your help.*

1.

"Bring them up!" the starter called.

I split away from the huddle of men leaning on the inside rail and jogged over to meet the first pair of horses coming toward the gate. The rider on the sturdy palomino passed me a thin leather strap that was slipped through the bit rings of the jigging dark bay beside her. "There you go, Reid. Good luck, Tracy."

The dark bay's rider nodded silently. Hustling to keep up with Marty, I glanced up at my mother's face under her helmet. She had her faraway look: everything tuned out except for the horse beneath her and the broad ribbon of dirt stretching away on the other side of the starting gate.

"Number one, please!"

I led the horse into the first stall, hopping up on a skinny ledge beside his head as the assistant starters slammed the gates shut behind him. "Easy, Marty, steady now, big guy," I murmured as he shifted restlessly. I slid the strap free of the bit, holding him steady by the bridle as Mom pulled down her goggles.

Voices called back and forth as one by one the rest of the field loaded into the starting stalls, metal gates clanging shut behind them. Around us the air crackled with tension.

My heart kicked into high gear, thumping against my ribs. My vision sharpened, and the bright colours of the silk blouses stretched across the backs of the jockeys intensified. I pulled in a long breath of air to slow my heart rate, reminding my body there was nothing to get ready for. I wasn't riding today, not a single race. Years of waiting had ended two weeks earlier, on my sixteenth birthday. I'd finally gotten my apprentice jockey's licence, only to find that on a circuit well supplied with experienced riders, no one wanted to ride a "bug."

Not even my mother.

Constant pestering got me named last weekend on a four-year-old maiden that hadn't won a race in two years of running. I'd royally screwed up the ride, breaking on my mount's mouth as he left the gate so he lost three lengths at the very start of the race. We finished third to last.

Without a mount in any race, I'd been hired on as

gate crew for the day. The big tracks had permanent staff working the starting gates. At smaller meets like this one, everyone pitched in.

Just a few horses left to load. Mom sat quietly in her tiny racing saddle, an aura of calm wrapped around her and Marty—alert, ready, *focused*. It was the hallmark of her success as a jockey: Tracy Widmark had nerves of steel.

The final horse was in. There was a brief silence. Marty's chin rested lightly on the front gate, his big thick ears at attention. I took another deep breath. "Good—" I began.

The gates sprang open and Marty burst out.

In two jumps he led the field, hugging the inside rail as the rest of the horses fanned out behind him. I leaped down from the gate and ducked under the rail into the infield, my eyes glued to the pack of horses as they swept past the screaming grandstand and into the first turn. Mom's bright blue-and-green silks were way out in front. I didn't need a stopwatch to know she was setting a blistering pace.

"What's she doing? That horse's gonna be all used up," complained Walt Fletcher, coming up to stand beside me.

I didn't say anything. Tracy Widmark was the leading rider on the circuit this year for a good reason. Anyway, Walt was always expecting the worst.

"He's through. They've caught him. He's done."

"The race isn't over yet," I said.

"Looks like it is for your horse," Walt predicted.

Sure enough, Marty had slowed enough to let two horses scoot past him. Over in the grandstand some of the spectators were yipping, cheering on a long shot as the field swarmed up on Marty's heels. Neck and neck, stride for stride, the two front-runners thundered down the back-stretch well ahead of the other horses, Marty falling farther and farther back as the field chased after the new leaders.

I set my face in a blank look. I jammed my hands into the hip pockets of my jeans so no one would see them trembling. My heart was racing with the horses. I let it go.

Coming out of the turn for home, the field scattered across the track. Marty stuck tight to the rail. Even as I crossed my fingers, hoping he'd hang on to make it to fourth or even third, Mom tucked in tight to his withers, her shiny blue arms pumping, urging our brave horse to go, go, *go*!

Marty exploded.

He pulled away from the field like he'd been shot out of a cannon. Legs churning, ears flat back and tail streaming, he charged up beside the leaders just in time to shove his big head in front as they passed under the wire.

A wave of cheering rolled out of the grandstand. I pounded the air with my fists and howled with joy.

"He won! He won!" Walt thumped me on the back,

nearly knocking me to my knees. I dodged out of reach and danced in circles like a fool.

Over on the track the riders were standing in their stirrups, pulling up their weary mounts.

"Oh my God!" Walt's paw caught my shoulder. "He's gone down!"

"Who? Who's down?" I whirled around, my eyes darting from horse to horse, searching for the familiar blue-and-green silks. They weren't there.

"Your mom's horse. Donny's mount ran right into him, knocked him off his feet."

I began running. The ambulance passed me. A large chocolate-brown mound lay on the track. Even as my brain admitted it had to be a horse, the mound heaved. Marty poked up his big, plain head and staggered to his feet.

I reached his side, pressed my hand against his sweaty neck, felt the heat. He stood squarely on all four feet. Alive, breathing, with four sound legs. I looked around for my mother.

"Okay, folks, move back. Give her some room."

As the ambulance attendants pushed back a small crowd by the rail, I caught a glimpse of bright blue. I shoved my way through.

Mom lay on her back beside the rail. Her eyes were open and staring. Her cheeks were as pale as the skim milk she used in her coffee. The attendant knelt beside her, bending down to examine the side of her head. I leaned over his shoulder and saw a dark trickle of blood in the white shell of my mother's ear.

"Mom! Mom, it's me, Reid. Can you hear me?"

"Someone get that kid out of here," said the attendant.

Hands grabbed my shoulders, pulled me back. I twisted away. "Marty! I've got to cool out Marty."

"Walt's got him, Reid," someone told me, I couldn't think who it was. "Don't worry, he'll look after him."

"Mom! Reid, where's Mom?" My little brother elbowed past people, runny nosed and grubby. "Is she okay?" He caught sight of our mother stretched out in the dirt and shrieked. I snagged his shirt collar and pulled him close. "We've got to stay back, Clem, while they take care of Mom."

"Let go! I want my mom!" Clement pounded my thigh with his fists. "Corky! Make him let me go!"

A jockey in dust-grimed silks settled his hands on my brother's shoulders. "Stop that right now, Clement. You got to behave." Corky's face, usually split in half with a big grin, was wrinkled with worry lines.

"But my mom…" Clement swiped at his nose, blinking rapidly.

Corky dried Clem's face with the red sleeve of his silks,

leaving streaks of dirt. "Your mom's hurt, son. These folks are looking after her. Best thing we can do is stay out of the way and let them do their job. Understand?"

Clement nodded, gulping back his tears. We watched as Mom was strapped onto a spine board and gently lifted into the ambulance. I felt Corky's strong hand grip my shoulder. I squeezed my eyes tight to ease the sudden stinging.

"Is she going to die?" Clement asked as the ambulance drove away.

Reaching across Corky, I cuffed my nine-year-old brother across the head.

2.

"Reid and Clement Widmark?"

I jerked awake in a hard chair to see a nurse in scrubs standing over me.

"You can see her now," she said.

Clement was already on his feet, running for the double doors leading into the intensive care unit. Corky and I came right behind him.

"I'm sorry, sir." The nurse held out her arm to block Corky. "Family only."

"I'm her brother," Corky lied.

We tiptoed through the ward to the last bed and stood side by side in a row, not daring to look at one another. Mom lay motionless beneath a blue blanket, her long braid of butter-blonde hair draped over one shoulder. Her arms were outside the covers, strapped and cuffed to a bank of beeping and blinking machines on the other side of the bed. A huge intravenous needle was taped to the inside of her elbow, a long thin plastic tube snaking to a bloated plastic bag of clear liquid hanging from a pole.

I took in the details of my mother's face—the high-set cheekbones and squared-off chin; the long, high-bridged nose that she'd passed on to me along with her fair colouring, except that my hair was just plain sandy, lacking her brilliant golden gleam. I saw the right features in the right places, but it was a face I barely knew.

Before anyone could stop him, Clement tugged at her hand. "Mom! Wake up, I'm here!"

A tiny line appeared between her eyebrows. Her eyelids flickered and slowly opened. Her dark green eyes stared at the ceiling, the frown creases deepening.

"Mom, look at me!"

Like a robot, Mom's eyes obediently slid toward us. They were blank and cool, like pebbles under water.

Burrowing his head under her hand, Clement nestled against her. Mom's fingers tangled in his soft dark hair. Her eyes brightened. "Clement," she croaked. She looked up. "Reid?" She sounded surprised to see us.

Corky leaned into her field of vision. "How're you feeling, girl?"

"Corky, what are you doing here?" She pushed her hands against the bed, started to sit up and dropped right back down, eyes clenched shut again. "Oh, my head aches."

"I'll get the nurse." Corky hurried away.

Mom opened her eyes again, scanning the IV pole and machines. "I'm in the hospital." She paused. "What happened?"

A nurse bustled in. "Ah, you're awake." She bent over Mom, placing a hand on her shoulder and looking into her eyes. "How do you feel?"

"Like I've been run over by a bulldozer. My head is pounding."

The nurse straightened and turned around. "I'm going to have to ask all of you to leave now. You can come back tomorrow."

Clement and I stayed in place beside Mom's bed.

"Come on, boys, your mother needs to rest," said the nurse.

We shuffled from the room. I stopped at the door. "See you, Mom. Take it easy, okay?"

"Goodbye, Reid. Bye, Clement," she said politely.

I caught Clement by the shoulder. "Say goodbye," I hissed.

He wrenched away and scooted out the door. He ran halfway down the hospital corridor before Corky reached him and pulled him close. "She's going to be okay, sport. It's just going to take some time."

"But she didn't want to hug us goodbye. She always wants to hug me."

Corky didn't even flinch as Clement rubbed his snotty nose against his shirt. "She's feeling pretty out of it right now. You get a hard bang on your head like she did, and it'll make you kind of dopey for a while. I've cracked my skull so many times it's amazing all my brains haven't leaked out." He fished a coin out of his pocket. "Here, go get yourself a pop."

Corky slung an arm around my shoulders as we watched Clement scuttle over to the vending machine squatting near the elevators. "Is your mom named on any of your horses tomorrow, Reid?"

"Tomorrow?"

"Are you running tomorrow?"

My own brain had stalled. I pushed it into gear, forcing myself to think about the Sunday races. "Singalong Susie in the second and Goingmyway in the fifth."

"Both your own horses. That's good. What about the others? Do you have any horses entered for your owners?"

I shook my head. "No, just our own two."

"Well, that makes things a bit easier."

"What do you mean?"

"Reid, you know what owners are like. They might have balked at riding a bug on their horses."

Finally I understood. Along with our own five horses, we trained four for outside owners. They had brought their horses to us because of Mom's skill and experience, and they expected that when they came to watch their horses run, she would be on board and not an apprentice jockey.

We were a small outfit, mostly making our way by running our own horses and living off their winnings. We raced in the bushes—on the B circuit, the second tier of horse racing. The purses weren't much, so we had to keep our expenses low. We did everything for the horses ourselves—feeding, mucking, galloping, hotwalking and, in Mom's case, riding in races. Mom liked it this way because she got to call most of the shots, which to her meant making the best decisions for the horses. Of course, a jockey can't be a trainer, not under the rules, so one of our owners, Walt Fletcher, was the paper trainer. Walt had the trainer's licence, and the horses were entered under his name, but everyone knew Mom was the real conditioner.

"Fletcher would give you the ride on his horse, but I don't think the others would," Corky went on. " 'Specially not old lady Rogers. Wouldn't make sense."

"I've been on Carmina before. The filly knows me."

"Galloping her in the morning once in a while is nothing

like riding her in a race, Reid. You know that."

I ducked out from under his arm. "The Lady Perthshire isn't until next Sunday. Mom will be back riding by then."

"Maybe." Corky shrugged. "Just…be prepared, okay?"

Before I could ask him what he meant, Clement was back, his brown eyes searching our faces like a lost spaniel puppy's. "I'm hungry," he whined.

"Then let's get you fed. What do you want to eat?" asked Corky.

"Spaghetti!"

"All right, spaghetti it is. Come on, Reid, let's go get something to eat."

I wasn't hungry and didn't want to go anywhere but back to the barn to check on our horses, just to reassure myself the edgy feeling in my gut meant nothing at all.

"Hurry up, Reid!" My little brother was already in the elevator with Corky.

Without any instructions from me, my feet carried me into the elevator. Hungry or not, maybe I needed a meal to clear the sour taste that had gathered at the back of my throat.

3.

My head wouldn't shut off that night, worries spinning around and around like a hamster in a wheel. After several hours it quit from sheer exhaustion; then I slept in and didn't get up until after five-thirty.

Hastily I kicked my legs into a pair of jeans and tugged on a T-shirt. A quick scrub with the toothbrush, socks and boots on and I was out the door of our travel trailer, a beat-up banana in hand to stave off hunger pangs. I let Clement sleep on.

Outside the air was sweet and cool. Sunrise was a pale lemon streak atop the mountains lining the valley. A couple of clouds littered the sky, giving me hope the day might cloud over and give some relief from the August heat.

I hurried through the campground to the backstretch.

The horses began yelling and banging their stall doors before I'd even turned the corner into our shed row.

"Okay, okay, settle down, you bunch of hayburners. Breakfast will be along in a moment." I went from stall to stall, checking in on each horse. When I'd made sure everyone was alive and healthy, I unlocked the feed room, which called forth another round of whinnying from the horse chorus. I set out the plastic feed buckets and began measuring grains and minerals and oils and salt into each bucket. I enjoyed this part of the job, playing the part of stable chef as I scooped and poured and mixed. The horses went delirious with joy as I emerged with the buckets loaded in a wheelbarrow.

I hooked a bucket inside each stall, starting with the star of the barn, Carmina. In true prima donna fashion she sniffed at her breakfast before daintily taking a mouthful. I resisted running a hand along her gleaming chestnut neck and left the stall. The princess did not care to be disturbed when she was eating. I couldn't help pausing for a few moments outside her stall just to look at her. I never understood why anyone would want to stand around looking at paintings and sculptures in stuffy old art galleries when there were horses as beautiful as Carmina to feast your eyes on.

Stall doors rattled under the impact of striking front

feet. I tore my gaze from the red filly and hustled down the shed row. The scent of brewing coffee drifted out of the tack room. I hung the last bucket and followed my nose.

"Morning, Reid," said Walt. He poured a mug of coffee and passed it to me. "How's Tracy?"

I took a sip of my black coffee and winced at the bitterness. Lying awake in the night I'd done a lot of thinking. Corky had given me a good clue about what could happen if word got around that Tracy Widmark wasn't going to be riding races for a while. I didn't have much information to pass along, but I was sure going to put a good spin on what I had. "Pretty good, Walt. We were up visiting her last night."

"She's conscious?" The creases over Walt's big nose smoothed out. "Well, that's good to hear. When's she getting out of hospital?"

I shrugged. "Soon, I guess. It's the weekend so it's hard to track down a doctor to find out."

"So it's nothing too serious?"

I took a gulp of coffee instead of answering. Walt went on.

"Leona Rogers called last night in a fuss. She'd heard about your mom. 'Course the main thing on her mind is who's going to ride her horse in the big race next Sunday. I told her—"

"Mrs. Rogers doesn't need to worry about Carmina. We'll get her to the Lady Perthshire."

Walt studied his coffee before heaving a sigh. "We'll talk about that later. Let's get through today first."

"Good idea." I tossed the rest of my coffee. "I've got to get horses out."

"I'll be right there," said Walt. He took his mobile phone from his pocket and left.

I pulled on my leggings and padded safety vest and stuffed my gloves in my hip pocket. I finished with my helmet, leaving the buckle dangling by my chin. I spent a few minutes carefully studying the wall chart outlining Mom's training plans for each horse in our little stable. Then, gathering my exercise saddle, a bridle, a set of rings and a plastic tote of brushes, I started tacking up the first horse of the day.

I was more disturbed by Mrs. Rogers' call to Walt than I'd let on. Leona Rogers didn't get out to the track much, mostly just on weekend afternoons when her horse was running, but she'd always seemed to be a really nice lady. I was surprised to hear she was more concerned about not having a jockey for Carmina in next Sunday's stakes race than about Mom's condition in hospital. It just didn't seem like her.

"Morning there, Reid." Corky's wrinkled-bag face

poked into the stall. "Got anything you need to get out?"

"Thanks, Cork, that'd be a big help. You mind taking Homer?"

"No problem. Is he ready?"

"I'll do him as soon as I'm done here." I briskly swiped a brush over Gracie, ignoring her legs and underbelly. I combed out her mane but left her thick black tail alone. Mom wouldn't approve, but then she wasn't here to notice, either.

I grabbed another set of tack and hustled down the row to Homer's stall. Corky was already inside, flicking the stable dust from the big horse's cocoa-brown back with a long-bristled dandy brush. "Thanks, Corky. I really appreciate this."

The old rider shrugged away my thanks. "Where's Clement?"

"Still sleeping."

Corky took the saddle and slid it into place on Homer's wide back. "You're going to need to hire some extra help."

I shook my head. "I can manage."

"You're going to ride all these horses, cool them out, feed and clean up after them, all by yourself? That's a big responsibility for a young fellow."

"I've been doing this work since I was littler than Clem. I can manage," I said again. "And Clement will help me."

"He's just a little kid. What about when school starts up? What are you going to do then?"

"That's weeks away. Mom will be back way before then."

Corky dragged his hand over his face, pulling all his wrinkles smooth. "I hope you're right, Reid. I sure hope you are right."

Walt showed up in time to boost us onto the horses' backs. As Gracie bounced underneath me, I dangled my legs down her sides, admiring the cinnamon-brown curve of her neck and the glossy black mane lying sleekly on one side. The filly felt alive and eager, happy to be going to the track. I let her good feelings seep into me.

Get up on the back of a good horse and you'll find yourself halfway to heaven. All your troubles and worries will be left behind, down at ground level, while you become part of a creature with more heart and courage, a more generous spirit, than any person has. A horse is the most genuine living being you'll ever meet. Hang around one, for just a few minutes even: you'll be a better person for it.

Gracie pranced through the gap onto the dirt track. I slipped my feet into the stirrups and bent my left knee to tighten the girth. Then I crossed my reins, checked to be sure Corky was ready to go, and released the filly into a trot. I stood high in my stirrups, keeping my weight right off her back.

We kept to the outside rail. A pair of workers blew past down on the inside. Corky jerked his head at the rangy grey pulling ahead of her work partner. "That's the filly Joel Mack claimed last month. Ice Storm. Pretty nice horse."

I had to agree. The grey had a fluid way of going that made her look like she wasn't putting out much energy at all in spite of the speed she was travelling. She was going to be a real contender in the Lady Perthshire Stakes.

That was good. Carmina liked to use her tremendous speed to go to the front, but if she was running all alone she tended to ease off, thinking she'd already beaten the other horses. Some serious competition would help keep her focused.

Passing the clubhouse, Corky called to me, "Let's go."

"Not yet," I shouted back. "Corky, wait!"

Too late. Corky had already moved Homer into a slow gallop. I gritted my teeth, annoyed he hadn't asked me for his instructions as he would have done with Mom.

Gracie fought against my hold, frustrated at being left behind. I let her go. A soft breeze tickled my cheeks as the horses picked up speed.

We sent the horses twice around the dirt oval, letting them pick up a bit of speed for the last two furlongs before pulling them up gradually. Corky and I faced our mounts to the infield, settling them for a few moments before turning around. We backtracked along the outside rail, the horses bobbing their heads on long reins. They were both blowing hard, but even as I listened Homer's breathing began to slow. I made a note on my mental list of things to tell Mom; she'd want to enter him for next weekend if there was a race for him.

Walt stepped out of our tack room when we came off the track. Clement was beside him, dressed in yesterday's grubby jeans, his T-shirt back to front. He was gobbling down a chocolate bar, and his eyes were puffy, as though he had just finished crying. Or was about to start.

I led Gracie into her stall, pulled off her tack and buckled on her halter. Calling to Clement to bring the scraper and sponge, I took her to the wash rack and hosed away the slime of sweat coating her neck and hindquarters.

"Is that what you're having for breakfast?" I asked, taking the thin plastic blade from my brother.

"You weren't there when I woke up." He made it sound like I'd deserted him instead of letting him sleep in.

"You couldn't make yourself a bowl of milk and cereal?"

"When are we going to see Mom, Reid?"

"As soon as we can get there."

"After you're done here?"

"There's racing this afternoon, Clem, remember? We've got two horses to run, and I've got to ride them."

I was busy thinking about what help I was going to need and who to get, so Clement's next words took a few moments to sink in. I had lifted the sweat scraper to slick water off Gracie's neck but just stood there, arm in the air. "What did you just say?"

"You're not going to ride Goingmyway. Corky is. Walt went to the office and changed riders."

"He had no business—" I shoved Gracie's lead shank at my brother. "Hang on to her." I stomped down the shed row, a glaze of red colouring my vision. "Walt!"

At my bellow he poked his head out of the tack room. "What's up, Reid?"

I stood in the open door, blocking it. Corky sprawled in the chair beside Mom's desk. "It'd better not be true."

Walt patted the air with his hands. "Now calm down, son. What are you talking about?"

"Did you change riders on our horses for today?"

"Of course I did. Your mom's not going to be riding so I had to—"

"Who did you name?"

"I put you on Singalong Susie, Reid, and…" He paused, his eyes sliding away. "Corky's going to ride Goingmyway."

I slammed my hand against the door jamb. "You had no right! They're our horses and I should be on them!"

"Reid, I *am* the trainer."

"That's just on paper, Walt, and you know it. It's not for real."

"It's real enough to make me responsible for those horses. Now, when you cool down enough, I know you're going to realize an experienced jockey's got a better chance of getting a horse to win, and that's what we're here to do"—Walt stabbed his finger at me—"win races."

"So why didn't you put Corky on both horses?"

The man himself answered. "Because I've already got a mount in the second, Reid, and I think she's a better horse than yours."

4.

My jaw dropped. I could feel it hanging open, but I couldn't seem to find the mechanism to snap it shut. I stared at this so-called friend of our family, the man Clem and I saw as an uncle or a grandfather, in complete disbelief. "How could you do this?" I spluttered at last.

"Look, you've been around this game all your life," said Corky. "You know what it's all about."

"Turning against your friends?" I said bitterly.

He shook his head. "It's about winning, Reid. That's all anyone here wants. I'm just putting myself in the best position to win."

I studied Corky hard, trying to make out what was different about him. What I saw was an aging professional athlete, body aching and stiff from a lifetime of injuries, hungry for one more big win.

I'd already started counting on Goingmyway giving me the first win of my career. The horse was a grinder, always trying his hardest but with only enough ability to win in the bottom claiming ranks. There wasn't much prestige in winning such a low-level race, and the jockey's share of the purse didn't amount to much. So why was Corky taking the ride away from me? With a flash of clarity I knew where this was all heading—to another horse in another race.

And in that same instant I made up my mind to do everything I could to stand in his way.

"Help! Reid, help me!"

I spun around in time to see Gracie yank the lead shank from Clement's hands and run the other way down the shed row. The shank smacked about her legs, frightening her. Cries of "loose horse" echoed through the backstretch. Gracie ducked around a corner and vanished from sight.

I sprinted after her, hoping, *praying*, she would come to no harm. So many things could happen to a panicked horse loose on the backstretch. She could slip and break a leg or collide with another horse or...

Gracie's head appeared, returning around the corner. Her ears were pricked, her eyes shining and alert, her footfalls even and rhythmical. She nuzzled the collar of the girl on the other end of her shank.

I was out of breath. Wheezing, I stuck out my arm, grasping for the shank.

The girl tightened her grip. "Does this horse belong to you?"

I nodded. My heart gave a funny kick against my ribs.

The girl's eyes were round. They were light brown, I noticed. A strange colour, like caramel candy. A colour I decided I liked.

The caramel-brown eyes were closer, just a few feet away. "Are you all right? Should I get help?"

I shook my head. My breathing was still quick and shallow. I forced in a lungful of air to slow it down. "I'm okay."

"Are you sure?" She placed her hand on my arm.

"Yes." Now my head was bobbing like it was coming loose from my neck. "I'm fine. Thanks for catching my horse."

"Oh, you're welcome." She took her hand away to stroke Gracie's neck. The filly sighed. I understood why: the girl had a real sweet touch. "I'm Ella Gervais."

"Hi."

"Hi." She arched her eyebrows. "And you are…?"

"I'm Reid Widmark."

She smiled and I felt another twinge in my chest. She had a nice open face with freckles over a nose that kind of tipped up at the end. Her hair was chocolate brown and shiny and tied back from her face in a bouncy ponytail that fell over her shoulder. Her cheeks were pink and getting pinker by the moment. She looked away, and I realized I'd been staring.

"Could I lead her back to her stall? I know how to handle a horse. I just don't have one anymore."

"Sure, if you'd like to. I'll stay close by, just in case."

"Of course. She's such a beautiful horse, she must be valuable. Aren't you, pretty lady?"

"Gracie. That's her barn name. She runs under Bright Grace. My mom named her."

"It's a lovely name." Ella patted Gracie again, and the filly practically fell to her knees.

The trip back to the shed row was somehow a lot shorter than it had been coming out. All too soon Ella was leading Gracie into her stall and turning her around in the correct way to face the door.

"Hold on to her for a moment, please," I asked. I knelt down and ran my hands over the filly's legs, probing for heat or swelling. There was nothing. I puffed my cheeks in a sigh of relief.

Ella slipped off the halter, and we stepped out of the filly's stall.

"I wonder..." She paused, twisting the halter in her hands.

Clement charged up, his cheeks smeared with chocolate. "Who are you?"

I cuffed him gently. "Don't be rude. This is Ella. She caught Gracie, so say thank you."

"Thanks," muttered Clement, scowling.

"You're very welcome." Ella smiled at Clem, pretending not to notice what a brat he was being. "And your name is?"

"I'm not supposed to tell strangers."

"His name is Clement," I told Ella.

"Reid, when are we going to see Mom?"

"Clem, I've got to do the horses first. Then we'll go to the hospital. But we won't be able to stay long because I have to get back for the races." I blew another sigh, remembering I still hadn't lined up any extra hands for that afternoon.

"Walt told me to tell you to wait until he's back before you take any more horses out," Clem said. "They're doing his horses first. He said you can start mucking out."

"Oh, he did, did he?"

"Can I help?" asked Ella. "I used to have a horse until… well, we moved down here. I don't know a lot about racehorses, but I can groom and clean stalls. I was in Pony Club up north before we left."

"That's a real nice offer, Ella," I said, liking the way her name just rolled off my tongue, "but I'd have to see if it's okay with my mom, and she's not here right now."

"Oh, sure." She jerked her shoulders in disappointment and turned to go.

"It's not that I can't use the help, because I can, and you'd do as good a job as anyone, better probably, it's just that..."

She looked back.

"Well, money's kind of tight with us right now. I don't know if we have enough to pay you."

Ella swung around, her cheeks pulled up in a big grin. She shook her head. "I don't want to be paid. I just want to be around horses again. I'd like to learn about racehorses, and you seem like a good person to teach me."

"The job's yours," I told her. I turned to Clem. "Help Ella, okay?"

"Why, what are you going to do?"

"Get the rest of the horses out."

"But Walt said—"

"Forget Walt. This is Mom's barn, and we're going to do things the way she wants them done."

5.

Ella was an angel.

She was a quick and efficient worker. Most important, she was comfortable with the horses. Thoroughbred racehorses at the peak of fitness are powerful, active animals with hair-trigger reactions. Ella had a good feel for them. She was kind and respectful, firm but not mean. She understood that horses aren't machines.

I showed her how to tack up, and we were soon into a routine. I'd take a horse out on the track. While I was gone, Ella would muck the stall. She even managed to sweet-talk Clem into picking up a fork and helping her. When I returned, she'd pull off the tack and get the next horse ready while I hosed the current horse. Then we'd trade horses, Clem legging me up while Ella walked the wet horse until it was cooled out and dry.

We were nearly done when Walt returned. The sun was well over the mountains and blasting heat like a furnace right through the clouds. I was glad to have only one horse left to get out.

Walt looked around. "I thought I told you to wait."

"What for, Walt?" I asked.

He frowned at me and rubbed his jaw. "So who's left?"

"Just the one, Walt," I said and led Carmina from her stall. Farther down, Ella brought out our pony horse, Keno. With only one horse left to do, I'd offered her a ride on the old horse in return for all her help. She'd eagerly accepted.

As I reached to pull down the stirrups, Walt took the filly's reins. "Thanks for getting her ready." Before I could protest, he led Carmina down the shed row, stopping at the end. Swearing under my breath, I scurried after them.

Corky and Leona Rogers came around the corner. For the second time that morning I felt the hinges on my jaw give way. I couldn't remember her ever coming this early in the morning to watch her horse train.

"Oh, there she is! My beautiful, gorgeous girl!" Mrs. Rogers cooed at her filly, her sandalled feet dangerously close to the filly's prancing hooves.

"Careful, Mrs. Rogers." I gently guided her back. "Carmina's full of herself this morning."

"Oh, Reid, I'm so sorry about your mother." She grasped my arm with fingers that felt like tiny bird claws. I haven't got much height to me, but even so, I was bending my neck to look down at her. Even at this early hour she was in full war paint, but beneath the mascara, eyeliner and cherry-red lipstick I saw real concern. "How *is* she?"

"Really good, Mrs. Rogers, thank you for asking."

"Such a brave woman. Really, I don't know how she does it. And such a gifted rider." She pressed her lips together and shook her head. "She understood Carmina so well."

"Mom *is* the best when it comes to figuring out how to get the most from a horse," I said, stressing the present tense.

Walt tossed Corky onto Carmina's back and took the filly's bridle to lead her. Carmina plunged forward, pulling him off balance, then bunny-hopped down the shed row, Walt hustling alongside to keep up. Waving to Ella and Clem to come along, I escorted Mrs. Rogers to the spectators' stand beside the track.

"What a beautiful horse," said Ella, parking Keno beside the stand as Carmina strode onto the track. She sat a horse well, relaxed and easy.

"Mrs. Rogers, this is Ella Gervais. Carmina belongs to Mrs. Rogers."

"Oh, you must be so proud of her. She's absolutely wonderful."

Leona Rogers beamed at Ella's admiration. "I am. She means a great deal to me. She's all I have left of my late husband. But I'm afraid she can be very naughty."

Carmina crab-stepped down the middle of the track, eyes rolling, amber tail lashing. Her thin ears flicked back and forth.

"Tracy does so well with her," Mrs. Rogers went on. "I don't know what I'm going to do now that she can't ride."

"Just for a few days, Mrs. Rogers. Mom will be back before you know it," I stated.

"Oh, Reid, that's such a relief to hear. Walter thought she might be out for weeks or even months."

I didn't say anything. I didn't know what to say or think. Were Walt and Corky just trying to look out for me and Clem until Mom got out of hospital...or were they taking advantage of our situation?

Out on the track Carmina's mincing steps were getting shorter and shorter until she was dancing on the spot. Her ears were plastered flat to her skull. She froze in her tracks.

"Oh boy," I muttered. Ella's eyes met mine over Mrs. Rogers' head.

Statue-like, Carmina stood rigidly in place. Corky rocked in the saddle, urging her to move. He chirped, scolded, pulled one rein and the other, before finally raising his whip.

"Don't do it, Corky!" shouted Clem. He slapped his hands over his eyes as the whip cut through the air and smacked the bunched muscles of the filly's hindquarters.

Carmina lifted off the ground. She reared, plunging forward, tearing the reins through Corky's hand. Her head dove down as she kicked her heels skyward, catapulting the jockey from her back. He rolled across the dirt as Carmina took off, running hell-bent for leather down the track.

I ducked under the railing of the stand and jumped down beside Keno. Without needing to be told, Ella had cleared out of the saddle on the far side. I vaulted into the big stock saddle, wheeling Keno around before my boots had found the stirrups.

Old Keno knew his job. He scooted to the gap and turned onto the track. Carmina was midway down the backside, tucked in tight to the rail like she was running a race, horses and riders scattering to get out of her way. Keno and I cut to the rail and waited for her to catch up to us.

Holding Keno in tight, I twisted around in the saddle, measuring the filly's approach. Her ears snapped forward as she sighted Keno in her path. She shifted her track off the rail.

I almost left it too late, deceived by her effortless way of going. She was nearly upon us when I let Keno loose. He was off like a shot, legs churning to bring us alongside the filly. Always a fighter, she responded by stretching out her giant strides.

Keno made it to her shoulder and hung there. I urged him on with my voice and body. He dug in and found a bit more, enough to move us up close enough for me to reach out and grab the reins flapping over Carmina's neck.

She made one attempt to yank free, testing my control of the situation, before adjusting her strides to match Keno's as he geared down to a trot. She wasn't too thrilled to settle to a walk, so I kept Keno at a jog. Even after running nearly a mile she was still bucking and kicking, so full of life she couldn't contain herself.

Feeling like a hero, I led her over to the gap where the others were clustered.

"Good work, Reid," said Walt. "Cool her out, will you please. Leona, you and I need to sit down and have a talk."

6.

"Can you tell us what room Tracy Widmark's in?" I asked the woman at the hospital reception.

She frowned at her computer. "Let's see…ah, there she is. She's been moved to the third floor. Room 326. Visiting hours are from two to eight."

It was ten in the morning. I had to be in the jocks' room by noon, a full hour before the first race. After the races were over, our barn of horses would need looking after, over an hour of feeding and watering and mucking out. We might make it back to the hospital before visiting hours ended if everything went smoothly at the barn, but a lifetime around horses had taught me to expect the unexpected.

Clement wasn't going to wait. "But I want to see my

mom now!"

That earned us a closer look. I could see the woman noting how short I was and deciding on my age—on the low side, of course. "You boys aren't here alone, are you? Where's your father?"

I dug my fingers into Clem's shoulders and steered him away from the counter. "We'll go get him."

"Reid, who're you going to get?" asked Clem.

"Nobody. I was just saying that."

"Where are you going?" He hurried after me as I marched down the hospital corridor, trying to look as if I knew exactly where I was headed.

"Here's the plan, Clem: we're going to find Mom's room and go in to see her."

"You mean we're going to sneak in?"

I nodded. "We don't want anyone to notice us, so we're going to have to be quiet. Got that?"

No answer. I looked down to see my little brother nodding vigorously, his mouth clamped shut.

We made it to the third floor without a problem. Room 326 was one over from the elevator. Boldly Clem and I went right in.

Mom was next to the window. She was propped up in bed with her eyes shut. They opened when Clem squeezed her hand. A smile spread slowly across her face. "Clemmie!

And Reid! How are my boys?"

"Good, Mom. We're doing just fine." I sat down in the bedside chair while Clem nestled his head against her like a puppy. "How are you feeling?"

She blinked hard. "Better. Just…a little fuzzy from time to time."

"When are you coming home?" asked Clem.

"Not for another few days, sweetie." She stroked his head.

"But you're awake now. Why can't you just come home?"

"The doctor wants me to stay a little while longer, just to make sure everything's okay." Her eyelids drooped and she made a visible effort to keep them open.

Two years ago, when Mom had gotten a concussion after her horse flipped in the starting gate, she'd been let out of hospital the next day. I studied her face with growing concern. She was unusually pale, with dark circles under her eyes.

"Are you boys doing okay?" she asked. "Are you eating good?"

I recalled Clem's chocolate-bar breakfast. "We're fine, Mom. You don't need to worry about us."

"I know, Reid, but I do. How's Marty?"

"He's fine. He came back good after the race."

"And the rest of the barn?"

"Pretty good. We got all the horses out this morning."

"Carmina dumped Corky on the racetrack," blurted Clem.

"What? What happened?" Mom sat up, her arms braced on the bed rails to hold herself steady.

"Corky gave her a swat, and she bucked him off. Then she ran all the way around the track until Reid caught her with Keno."

I yanked Clem's T-shirt to shut him up. "She's okay, Mom. Not a scratch on her. She was just running for fun."

"Why on earth was Corky on her?"

Clem squirmed out of my reach. "Walt told Mrs. Rogers that Reid was too green to ride her. He said Carmina's been getting away with murder and needs an experienced rider on her to straighten her out."

"Mom, what are you doing?" I asked anxiously.

She shoved the bedcovers aside and pitched forward, nearly falling out of bed. I caught her arm and held her steady.

"I've got to talk to Walt."

"Just lie down again, please. You tell me what you want to say, and I'll make sure it gets to him."

She flopped back on the pillows. "You know the horses, Reid, and what needs to be done with them. Tell him that. Tell him I've put you in charge of the barn."

"Sure, Mom, I'll do that." Privately, I wondered if Walt Fletcher would listen to anything I said.

"Walt's a good friend. So is Corky. They're just trying to help." Mom's eyelids sank down.

"Sure they are," I agreed.

"Well, now, what's going on here?" A nurse came into the room. "Who are these fine young men, Tracy?"

"My sons, Reid and Clement," Mom murmured, eyes still closed.

The nurse wrapped her fingers around Mom's wrist, taking her pulse. "Head still aching?"

Mom nodded silently.

"Boys, you're going to have to go for now while I look after your mother. You can come back later, during visiting hours. Don't you worry, we're taking good care of her."

"I'm hungry. I want something to eat," said Clem as we crossed the hospital parking lot to the truck.

"We'll be home in a few minutes."

"There's nothing to eat at home. You didn't get groceries."

"Like I've had time to go shopping. You can have a peanut butter sandwich." I opened the truck doors and rolled down the windows to let out the sweltering heat before getting in.

"There's no bread."

"Give me a break, will you, Clement!" I adjusted my seat pillow and jammed the key in the ignition. "Do up your seat belt."

Clem muttered something rude under his breath.

"What did you say?"

"Nothing." He slumped against the seat, his face pressed into the side window.

I turned over the ignition and shoved the truck into reverse. My foot stomped down on the accelerator and the truck shot backward. A horn blared. I hit the brake and a car dodged around us.

I let my head drop onto the steering wheel with a bang.

"You okay, Reid?" asked Clem.

I heaved a sigh and sat up. "Yeah. How about you?"

No answer. I looked over. Clem snuffled, wiping the back of his hand under his nose. I reached over and gently thumped his shoulder.

"Hey, it's going to be all right. You know what? I'm hungry too. We'll pick up some burgers on the way back to the track." I backed the truck up again, carefully this time.

"Salad. You'd better have a salad. Grilled chicken with it, maybe, but no dressing. Remember, you're riding races this afternoon."

"Oh, I remember, Clem."

"Reid, how come you didn't tell Mom that Corky took over the ride on Goingmyway?"

"Well, I never really got a chance to."

"Do you think Mom forgot we've got horses running today? Because she didn't say anything about the races."

"She would have if that nurse hadn't come in and made us leave. Look, Clem, don't fret about Mom. She's going to be fine."

"Promise, Reid? You really think so?"

"Yes, I do."

"Cross your heart and hope to die?"

"Can't, little bro, I'm driving. Got to keep both hands on the wheel."

Clem said nothing until we stopped at a red light. "Cross your heart?" he repeated.

Feeling like a liar, I made the sign of the cross on the left side of my chest. "Mom's going to be fine." I hesitated, then added, "I swear it."

Clem puffed out a long sigh.

I glanced over and was relieved to see the old-man worry lines were gone from his forehead. I wasted a few seconds wishing I was a little kid again.

The light changed to green. I put both hands back on the wheel again, let out the clutch and switched my brain to a more useful activity.

Let it be so, I prayed. *Let Mom be all right.*

An hour before the first race, I was in the jocks' room pulling on thin white breeches and tall black boots. I shrugged on the padded vest that protected my upper body, but I left it undone. I set my tiny five-pound racing saddle with its two girths out for the valet and went to join the other riders on some tree-shaded benches at the side of the paddock.

"Hey, Reid, how's Tracy?" asked Corky right away.

"Pretty good." I didn't bother wondering how he knew we'd gone to see her. Gossip runs around a racetrack faster than most of the horses.

"So when's she getting out?"

I shrugged. "Tomorrow sometime. Got to wait for some paperwork to get done." My lies sounded weak to my own ears.

Corky raised his eyebrows and looked away. I spared a moment to wonder what was going on inside his head, then got on with the things I had to say.

"Mom says thanks for helping us out. So do I."

"You're very welcome, both you and Tracy." He slung an arm around my shoulders. "Anything for my good friends."

I twisted my head and looked him right in the eye. "She wants me to tell you that she's put me in charge of the barn."

"Has she now?" His arm squeezed my shoulders hard and dropped. "Well, that's a lot of responsibility for a young fellow like you to carry all by yourself."

"I know the horses. I know how Mom wants things done."

Corky nodded, bobbing his head in agreement to every

word I said. "You're Tracy's right arm, Reid; it makes sense she'd want you doing your horses."

"*All* the horses, Corky. I'm in charge of all the horses in our barn."

"Whoa, now, son." Corky rocked back on the bench. "I don't think that's the way it can be."

"It sure as heck can. That's the way Mom wants it, and she's the trainer."

"*Is* she now? Seems to me last time I looked, Walt Fletcher's name was down as trainer."

Our rising voices were turning heads our way. I forced my voice low. "That's just on paper, Corky, and you know it. Mom's the real trainer."

"Let me ask you a question, Reid: do you have your trainer's licence?"

"You know I don't."

"That's right, you don't, and you can't run horses without one. Walt Fletcher does. That puts him in charge."

"What are you saying, Corky?"

"Your horses are your business, but it's up to Walt and Leona Rogers and the other owners to decide what's best for their horses."

A wave of heat flushed through me. "You lousy—"

"Careful, boy, watch your language." He gestured to the crowd gathering outside the paddock fence. "You don't want to get yourself a fine from the stewards, now, do you?"

What I wanted was to wipe the grin off his leathered face. I forced my clenched fists open, clamped my fingers over the edge of the bench and leaned in close. "You're trying to steal the ride on Carmina. You want to be on her in the Lady Perthshire."

"Sure I do. Who wouldn't? The filly's got a real good chance."

"So you admit it!"

"Settle down, Reid, you're jumping the gun. Tracy's still got the ride on the filly."

"That's right, so you just stay away from our horse."

Corky looked me full in the face for what seemed like a long time. "The filly can't stay in her stall until the Perthshire. Someone's got to gallop her in the mornings until your mom gets back."

"That someone's going to be me."

"Get real, kid. No one hands over a stakes-calibre filly to a bug with a brand new licence." He shook his head. "Not when there's an experienced jockey available."

"You're supposed to be our friend!" I said bitterly.

"I am, son. I wouldn't be wasting my breath telling you all this if I wasn't. You're playing with the big boys now. No one's going to step aside to let you into this game. You've got to prove yourself, just like we all did."

7.

Hunched over on the bench, I watched horses stride around and around the paddock, my chest on fire.

"Nervous, kid?" asked the jockey sitting beside me. I followed his eyes to my trembling hands.

"No, Sammy." I clasped my hands together. "I'm not nervous." I took a couple of deep breaths. The heat inside me died away, replaced by an icy calm. Suddenly my vision was more clear, my focus sharper.

Coolly, I watched as the horses in the first race were saddled and the riders thrown up. The crowd pressed up against the fence, three to four people deep, fanning themselves with tipsheets and programs against the heat. The paddock gate swung open and the horses pranced onto the track, partnering with their ponies to parade past the grandstand. The fans drifted away, back to their seats in the stands or to positions along the rail.

I returned to the deserted jocks' room and double-checked my gear, impatient for the first race to be over so preparations for the second could begin. I paced the narrow length of the room, swatting the air with my whip. I followed the progress of the race outside by sound: the peal of the starting gate bell, screams from the fans, the thunder of hooves.

Soon, I thought, *very soon.*

The announcer blared the winner—Corky's mount, of course. I slipped into our blue-and-green silks and picked up my helmet. The other riders stomped into the room, sweating and swearing. I sat down right next to the fan, my elbows propped on my knees and my helmet cupped in my hands. The whir of the fan blades drowned out the buzz and bustle around me. I fixed my eyes on the toes of my boots.

"Hey, son, you praying over there in that corner? Asking God to grow some wings on that filly you're riding?"

I didn't look up to see who was taunting me.

"Leave him alone," growled Corky.

"Hey, chill, old man. Just having a little fun. You know, lighten things up in here."

"You bet I'm praying," I said. I lifted my head and looked

my heckler right in the face. It was Tonio Juarez, a seasoned rider who'd gone nowhere in his career. "I'm going to do whatever it takes, *everything* it takes to win this race."

"Hey, look out, here comes the kid," hooted Sammy.

The wisecracks and teasing continued until the call came.

I trooped out to the paddock with the other riders. Following tradition I shook hands with Walt before he boosted me onto Susie's back. I gathered up the reins and slipped my feet into the stirrups. As the filly was led onto the track, I quickly scanned the crowd. Right away I spotted Ella and Clem, both of them waving hard in my direction.

I didn't have a lot of fans yet, but the two I had were real good ones.

I nodded a greeting to Susie's pony rider as he picked us up. I could feel the filly bottling up underneath me, so I told the pony rider to trot. Susie plunged ahead, dragging her head down, protesting being restrained. An experienced runner with more heart than ability, she was both eager and anxious for the race to get underway.

"Hey, hey, sweet girl, take it easy," I crooned. "It's going to be good, real good." I stood high in my stirrups, bracing my hands on her neck. Her stride smoothed out, her tension easing.

We passed in front of the grandstand. The announcer called out our names, but I didn't hear a thing. I was aware only of the narrow brown filly trotting beneath me, her short black mane fluttering on top of her long neck.

"Want to lope now?" asked the pony rider.

I shook my head. "We're fine."

"You sure?"

"I am," I told him. And I was. We trotted until Susie's tight, crabbed-up stride stretched out and she quit fussing with her head. Then the starter called and we headed toward the gate.

Walt came up and took the filly from the pony rider. "How's she feel?"

"Great. Really great." I only had to half fake the confident grin I shot down at him. "She feels like a winner today." I pulled down my goggles.

Walt couldn't mask his look of disbelief. With a shrug of his shoulders he walked Susie around in circles as the first four horses entered the gate.

"Five horse!"

Susie's head tossed as Walt led her into the narrow starting stall. "Quit that, you," he growled as he lumbered up onto the pontoon beside her swinging head.

I sat chilly, counting off horses out of the corner of my right eye as they entered the gate. When the nine horse was in, I took up my reins, grabbed a hank of mane and braced my left foot forward.

When the gates flew open, Susie was still fighting Walt's efforts to position her. All around us horses charged forward. Susie scrambled awkwardly after them, her head cocked, her path skewing into the horse beside us. I was with her, holding hard on her left rein to pull her clear. Her shoulder rubbed up against the six horse's rump as she struggled to find her balance.

"Get off us! Get over!" screeched the six jockey.

Susie's stride was levelling, her front legs reaching out to pull her slender frame over the ground, her head and neck tipped left. I eased up on the rein and she pulled ahead, drawing clear of the other horse.

In front of us the field clung to the rail, saving strides by taking the shortest route around. Our slow break had left us out of that game. I positioned Susie one out, her long effortless stride picking off horses one by one. She had one pace and she was in it. There would be no handy turn of speed coming down to the wire to carry us past the front-runners. Our only chance was to run them down.

Going into the clubhouse turn, we were six off the pace and slowly gaining. The race was a long one, a mile and a sixteenth. We still had a good way to go. Susie was galloping easily, ears pricked, her big stride carrying us up through the field bit by bit.

Halfway down the backstretch we stalled, holding our position but running in place. The impulse to send her on, to ask her to run harder, put out more, was almost overwhelming.

Wait, I told myself. *It's too soon.*

Or was it? We were angling into the second turn, riders shifting their hips to the outside as their mounts leaned into the corner. Susie had to be within striking distance of the front-runners as we came down to the wire. Then we had to hope they would tire, their energy spent after leading the race this far, enough so that Susie's limited speed could carry us past them.

We moved up, fifth place, then fourth. A single horse ran along the rail three lengths in front of us. Way ahead two runners duelled it out, a long empty stretch of track between them and the third-place horse.

Susie's stride felt steady and regular. I still had lots of horse under me.

The gap behind the front-runners was vanishing. The horses were tiring, their jockeys riding hard to keep them together for these final strides to the wire. All around us riders whooped and hollered, urging their mounts on in the run to the finish.

I chirped to Susie, tucking in tight to her withers and

shouting her on. I felt her respond, her body dropping down as she reached out her stride even longer. Her ears flattened to her skull with the effort. We easily passed the third-place horse.

The front-runners were coming back to us. Just a few more strides and Susie would have them. They split apart and I aimed her at the gap between them.

Down on the rail, a horse exploded. Legs churning like pistons, she flew past us all. Her jockey punched his fist in the air as they passed under the wire, certain of his mount's victory.

I didn't quit, pushing Susie with my body and my voice, calling to her, asking for all she had.

Body straining, she gave it, her every stride pulling us farther and farther up into the gap. The three horses were running in unison, matching strides, so close a blanket could have covered us. In a tightly packed trio we swept through the finish.

8.

The race was over, but Susie still wanted to go. I let her gallop out up to the turn, mostly because I didn't have the energy to pull her up.

It took the last reserves of my stamina to stand in the stirrups, my upper body acting as a counter lever to Susie's forward momentum. My muscles were turning to jelly, but I resisted the urge to suddenly jerk her to a walk, mindful of the strain a sudden decrease in speed would place on the vulnerable tendons and ligaments of her limbs. I was starting to wobble when the filly finally consented to slow down. She broke to a trot and I turned her around, hustling her back to the stands to find out where we'd ended up.

I was gasping for air like a dying fish, breathing so hard I couldn't hear the race announcer until we were in front of the grandstand.

"—hold all tickets pending a steward's inquiry into the running of the last race."

Walter hurried onto the track and took Susie by the bridle. "Tim Corrigan claimed foul against you for bumping him at the start. Don't worry, it'll come to nothing; he finished seventh."

I vaulted off Susie and pulled off my saddle. "Thanks, girl, you ran good." I patted her chest and she responded by rubbing her sweaty head against my shoulder, nearly knocking me over. Walt led her down the track to the gap while I walked briskly along the outside rail, in line with the other jockeys to weigh out.

I forced a grin on my face, my head turned to the crowd and away from the winner's circle where a hard-blowing horse was circling.

"The results of the second race have been declared official! In first place…"

I stepped onto the scale with my saddle.

"Land's End with Corky Sinclair aboard. In second place, Brand New Day. Third, by a nose, Aggravation. Also by a nose, in fourth place, Singalong Susie."

The clerk of the scales gave a nod. "Good race, Reid."

"Thanks." I hopped off, marching back to the jocks' room like I had another race to ride. I darted one quick glance over my shoulder.

Land's End posed in the winner's circle with her groom at her head, her owners and all their friends clustered beside her, her jockey's face wrinkled in a huge smile as the photographer took the picture, preserving the moment of victory for years to come.

The clerk of the scales was right: I had ridden a good race. My horse had run her heart out for me, given me everything she had—but Susie's everything had just been enough to get us to fourth place.

I was never going anywhere as a jockey without good horses to ride.

I was still in the jocks' room when Randy Sirwah hobbled in. He'd come off his mount leaving the gate, spraining his ankle, or so he claimed. I caught the look in his lowered eyes, though, and it was fear.

He sat down, studying the backs of his hands as if the wrinkled skin outlined a treasure map. "Hey, kid, you want my rides?"

"Seriously?"

He nodded, still looking down. "You can have them all. Every race but the last."

The stakes race, the big race of the day where the really good horses would be run. It was a short field, only six horses entered, leaving some jockeys, the unpopular and unproven, without mounts.

"Forget his ride in the fifth, Reid. That horse is crazy." Corky crossed the room to stand over us.

"Who are you, the kid's agent?"

"Just looking out for him. He doesn't need to be riding any nutcase horse."

"Sure that's all you're doing, Corky? That 'nutcase' horse has got some run in him. Maybe you're worried the bug here might just beat you on him."

"Quit trying to stir up trouble, Sirwah," said Corky.

Randy went on. "You know, why don't you give the kid his momma's horse back and *you* can take my mount? That'd be the fair thing, don't you think?"

Corky sat down and stretched back in his chair, yawning, showing how bored he was with the whole conversation.

"So what do you want to do?" Randy asked me.

"I'll ride," I said. "All of them."

If Corky had stayed out of it, I might have turned down Randy's offer. Not one of his mounts had a snowball's chance in hell of winning, and that's what I needed to make my reputation as a rider: winners. I still wanted to believe Corky meant well, but he had to quit messing with my life. It was time to take a stand, so I accepted the rides.

And I did a good job on each and every one of them.

Managed to place third on the horse in the fifth, even after he blew up in the gate and had to be reloaded. Goingmyway won, of course, with Corky aboard. As the owners of Goingmyway, we would receive sixty percent of the purse money. I reminded myself of that several times, trying to overcome the resentment burning in my guts.

Showered and changed, I watched Corky run second by a neck on Charlene Abrams' gelding in the last race. Then I staggered back to the barn on rubbery legs for evening chores.

Ella and Clement were already there, stuffing hay nets and filling water buckets. I propped myself against a wall. "Hey, you guys."

"Reid! Oh, you were wonderful!" Ella seemed to sparkle, golden light glinting off her dark brown hair in the evening sun.

"You rode pretty good," Clement seconded.

"I did, didn't I?"

"Everything's just about done here," Ella said, picking up a bulging hay net and slinging it through the eyebolt at the front of Carmina's stall. I hurried to help her.

"She's a beautiful horse," Ella sighed. "Look, she's hugging you."

Carmina had set her head over my shoulder and pulled me close. I rested my forehead against her bony cheek. "If you're ever feeling down, let Carmina give you one of her special hugs; that'll cheer you right up."

"Are you feeling down, Reid?"

I shrugged, trying to find words for the unsettledness in me. "No, just…frustrated."

"Want to tell me about it?"

I turned around and wrapped my hands over Carmina's white blaze, tucking her long head into my chest. I could see Ella now, her caramel-brown eyes warm and kind, and I liked what I saw. "May I take you out to supper?"

She smiled and nodded. "That would be nice."

"That's all you get paid?" Ella asked. She blinked her eyes in disbelief. "You risked life and limb to make a few dollars?"

I speared a leaf of lettuce—no dressing, just salt and pepper—and nodded. "Jockey fees are nothing. You've got to ride a winner to make any money. You see, a winning horse gets sixty percent of the purse, and the jockey gets ten percent of that."

"Well, it's simple, then: you need to ride winners. You'll do it, Reid. You're an amazing rider."

My face felt warm. "Tell the trainers that."

"Can't they see?"

"The thing is, there's lots of experienced, proven jockeys on the circuit right now. Naturally the trainers are going to ride them on their good horses."

"But how do you get to prove yourself unless they give you a chance?"

"Well, that's the problem. I'm just lucky we've got our own horses."

"You'll ride them and win. And once you've proven what a great rider you are, you'll move on to better and better horses."

I nodded. She understood completely. "Good riders get good horses and more chances to win races. It's a magic circle."

I munched my salad thoughtfully. Talking to Ella reminded me my future was on track. Riding those no-hopers in today's races had just been a minor glitch in the Plan.

"I'm going to ride at the big tracks, Ella. In the top races. The Queen's Plate and the Kentucky Derby. The Epsom Derby and l'Arc de Triomphe. All of them."

She tipped her head, studying my face. "I know. I know you will."

She had a way of making me feel I'd suddenly grown a whole foot taller. My cheeks bunched up, pulling my mouth into a grin, while I looked right back at her, enjoying the view. Each time I looked, there was something new to see in her face. This time I noticed that the freckles sprinkled over her nose looked like flecks of cinnamon. "What about you, Ella? Tell me all about yourself."

"My life's pretty ordinary compared to yours. I have a brother and a sister, both younger than me and total brats. We just moved down here from up north at the beginning of summer. My parents are working for my uncle in his janitor business. Dad's mill shut down, and he was out of work for a long time. We had to sell everything." She paused to take a deep breath. "Including my horse."

"That must've been rough."

She nodded. "It was. I had Timber for six years. I bought him myself, but there was no way we could afford to keep him. We had our own land back home, but here we just have a house, so I would have had to board him out and it would be just too expensive."

Her eyes were shiny. She squeezed them shut, holding back tears. I covered her hand with mine.

"I'm sorry," she whispered. "I just really miss him."

"We'll get him back. A couple of wins and I'll have enough to buy him back for you."

"Oh, Reid, that's so nice of you, but I still wouldn't have a place to keep him. I'm working as a cashier at the liquidation store for the summer, but my parents want me to save all that money for college."

"So we'll train Timber to pony horses. We can use

another pony horse; Keno's not young anymore. Timber can earn his keep and live at the racetrack. You can come and ride him there." My brain was really firing, brilliant ideas flying out of it like sparks. "I'll show you how to pony horses on him—you'll learn quick—then you can make a few extra dollars on race days."

Her eyes opened wide. "You really think I could do that?"

"I know you can, Ella. You're a good hand around horses."

"Oh, Reid, that would be a dream come true, getting Timber back *and* working around horses. You're a wonderful person, do you know that?"

I ducked my head, trying to act modest, although my spine felt like it had suddenly stretched out another foot. At this rate I was going to have to quit race riding and take up basketball.

"What about your mother, Reid? Will this be okay with her?"

Good question. "She'll be good with it. Like I said, we're going to need another horse to take over from Keno one day. Better sooner than later." I wasn't quite as certain that Mom would approve my plan as I pretended, but saying so might risk disappointing Ella and taking away all of that sparkly happiness.

We finished our meal with me telling Ella about every horse in the barn. Especially Carmina.

"She's probably the most difficult, frustrating horse that was ever foaled," I said. "I'm sure she stays up all night in her stall dreaming up ways to drive the people around her crazy. Three trainers gave up on her before Mrs. Rogers brought her to us."

"What does she do?"

"Everything! Bucks, rears, runs away with her rider. That filly's got so much energy she just can't contain herself. She's always got to be doing something. In the morning she'll watch every horse leave the shed row and come back; I swear she counts them. If you're brushing a horse in the next stall, she'll rear up to look over the wall and see what you're doing. She amuses herself with little games: flopping her lips or sticking out her tongue. She's got definite opinions about how she wants to be treated. You've got to go along with her, make her think that what you want her to do is really her idea, because she's also got a powerful drive to win, and you don't ever, ever want to turn that against you."

"Like Corky did today."

"Exactly. You see, a lot of people at the track think we spoil her, let her get away with too much. Of course, they've never been on her back, like Mom and I have."

Ella leaned across the table, propping her elbows to rest her chin in her hands. "Tell me what it's like to ride her."

"My mom rides her mostly, so I haven't been on her a lot. But those times...well, it was like..." I took a few moments, finding the right words. "Like sitting on a hurricane. You're only there because she allows you to be. Because she wants to share her speed and power with you. She loves to run; you saw that this morning. She just loves it. But you don't ever want to get her riled up, because once she's made up her mind she's not doing something, it's a big fight to change her mind."

"How many races has she been in?"

"Just two. She ran a close second in her first start for another trainer, and she won her second for us by five lengths last month, with Mom aboard."

"And your mom's going to ride her in this big race next weekend?"

I pasted on a confident smile and nodded. Suddenly I was weary, all my energy drained away as though a plug had been pulled. I let the smile fall off.

Ella noticed. "Come on, you're tired. It's time to go."

"I have to pick up Clem before he drives the neighbours crazy."

"It's so nice the way everyone on the backstretch is helping you out."

"They're pretty good people," I said. The couple in the motorhome beside us had agreed to look after Clem for the evening before I'd even finished asking. More examples of assistance tumbled through my mind: Corky turning up to gallop; Ken and Mandy cooling out our horses after the races and refusing to be paid; even Walt trying to step into Mom's shoes as the trainer. I rubbed my chin, thinking I must have been a little sun crazy to suspect Walt and Corky of taking advantage when all they'd done was give me a hand.

I paid the bill, and we went outside into the soft August night.

"I can't wait to meet your mom," Ella said, rolling down the pickup's window as we drove along the city streets to her house. "She sounds like an amazing woman."

"She is."

"Is she...on her own?"

"Yes, except for Clem and me. My father took off when I was little."

"I'm sorry," said Ella.

I shrugged. "Don't be. I don't even remember him." I had never missed him, either. Corky had been more of a father than the man who'd sired me; well, at least until recently. "Clem's dad is Bryant Hughes. He was a jockey too. He and Mom were married, but they got divorced when Bryant moved back to Saskatchewan to farm. He was a decent rider, but he got real heavy and couldn't do the weight."

"Your mother didn't go with him?"

"No, the racing's lousy in Saskatchewan. They're still good friends, though."

Ella went quiet for a while. "Riding racehorses meant that much to her?"

"You bet it does."

"Just like you, huh?"

"That's right. Race riding is everything in the world for me. I'm going to the top, Ella, and I'm not going to let anybody or anything sidetrack me from getting there."

She was quiet, which made me wonder what she was thinking. After a while she said, "Turn left at the next street. Slow down, there, that's our house, the one with the porch light on."

I pulled over in front of a plain two-storey with a carport at the side. Ella slid out before I turned off the truck. "How about I come early tomorrow and give you a hand before I go to work?"

"That'd be great, Ella, but you don't have—"

"I want to. It's fun. See you in the morning." She shut the door and skipped up the sidewalk, pausing at the front door to give me a last wave before vanishing inside.

9.

I woke up the next morning before my alarm with everything clear in my head.

I saw my life laid out like a road map with my destination—the winner's circle—marked with a big black X. A lot of roads led to that X, some of them winding and stopping at other places along the way, others going straight through. Then there were the roads that started out going in the right direction, only to veer off and go nowhere. I had to be careful to avoid going on those.

I needed to get on the most direct route—the freeway— and I had a plan to get there.

I kicked off the bedcovers and rolled out of bed, stretching my cramped muscles. I made a mental note to get fitter.

"Wake up, Clem." I reached up to the bunk above mine

and shook my little brother's shoulder. "Let's go."

He swatted at my hand. "Leave me alone. I'm sleeping."

I took hold of his ankle and pulled him out of bed. He squealed and slapped at my hand, but I showed no mercy. "You've got to get up. I need your help."

"No way!" He wrenched free. "I'm going back to bed."

"Clement, I'm not telling you again. You're going to help me. Now get dressed." I was doing just that as I spoke. By the time I'd combed my hair and brushed my teeth, Clem was back in his bunk, the covers pulled over his head. "Okay, have it your way." I shoved my feet into my boots and propped open the trailer door. I tucked Clem's boots under my arm. Then, reaching around the blankets, I grabbed my little brother around his middle and packed him outside.

Trapped inside the blankets, Clem's arms and legs flailed uselessly. His lungs still worked good. He screeched like a car alarm, setting doors slamming on nearby trailers and voices calling out all the way to the barns. I dropped him and the boots outside the tack room and dug my fingers into his collarbone. "Listen up now."

"You're hurting me!"

"Too bad." I gave him a shake. "Put your boots on."

"No way."

I shook him again. "So help me, Clement, do it!" I let him go and retrieved the tack room key from its hiding place.

"You're crazy, Reid, you know that?"

"That's right, I am, so don't mess with me." I zipped up my leggings, shoved on my helmet and hoisted Keno's stock saddle off the stand. I tacked up the old gelding and brought him over to Clem. "Get your helmet."

"What are you doing?"

I gave him the reins and didn't answer, heading back into the tack room for another set of tack, this time an exercise saddle and bridle. I packed the tack to the stall next door and ducked under the webbing of the stall guard.

"Does Walt know you're going to ride her?"

I smoothed the saddle cloth on Carmina's broad chestnut back and gently settled the saddle in place. "Nope."

"But—"

"I'm doing this, Clem, so shut up." I slipped the bit in the filly's mouth and lifted the headstall over her tapered ears. I buckled the straps and tidied her forelock under the brow band. I saw my reflection in miniature in those huge dark eyes. For a few moments I leaned my forehead against the wide bone that was her cheek. "Make me big, lovely lady. Please. You can do it. Make me a big rider."

She sighed, a long rush of air. Her feet shifted restlessly and she bunted my shoulder.

"Okay, okay, we'll get going." I unsnapped the stall guard and led Carmina out.

My little brother legged me up, then climbed onto an overturned bucket to get on Keno. Side by side we went through the shed rows in the grey morning light and onto the track.

"Stay with me, okay?" I muttered to Clem. The filly's ears were twitching like a rabbit's. I could almost hear the gears turning in her head.

"Reid, are you sure you should be riding her without telling Walt?"

"Walt's got nothing to do with this horse."

"He's the trainer!"

"No, he's not. Mom is."

"But Mom's not here right now."

"I know that, Clem. I also know she put me in charge of the stable. You were there; you heard her say so."

"I think you shouldn't do this, not without Walt knowing."

I tuned him out. Right now there was nobody in the world but myself and the edgy red filly underneath me. Those big black eyes rolled back, looking right at me. Her neck came up and her long tail lashed back and forth. I chirped to her, encouraging her to keep going, and tapped her shoulder lightly with my stick. She shook her head and ducked away, offended.

I held the rein, stopping her from turning right around.

She swung her head, attempting to wrench the rein free, but I held firm. Clucking and chirping and rocking, I managed to get her to travel across the track on a diagonal path. We reached the outside rail and I took hold of the opposite rein, guiding her the other way. "Clem, get up with me!"

"What the heck are you doing? Why don't you just keep her straight?"

I ignored his questions and kept zigging and zagging Carmina across the track. Her bunched-up stride was stretching out, and those slender ears had settled into a forward position. "Good filly," I crooned. "You're the best, Carmina, a superhorse."

We could never have travelled like this if there'd been other horses on the track: our crooked, winding route would have had us cutting off traffic, maybe even colliding with a horse or two. But it worked. As we wound our way up the track past the spot where she'd managed to get rid of her last rider, Carmina's resistance became half-hearted and then just fell away. I felt her rib cage expand in a huge sigh, as if she too was relieved to have left that difficult area behind.

On her own, Carmina picked up the pace and broke into a lope. In two strides we'd left Clem and Keno behind. It didn't matter. I had felt it the moment the filly had switched her attention. She revelled in the pleasure of moving her giant body over the earth simply by swinging her long stick legs back and forth. The motion was effortless, graceful, magnificent. She was a force of nature, creating her own wind that pushed at my cheeks and stung my eyes. I was laughing, but the sound was torn away from my mouth.

Crouched low on her withers, my body rocked to the rhythm of Carmina's big stride. My arms reached forward, more and more, as she reached for more ground. The racetrack was still empty, not a horse in sight, yet Carmina galloped as hard and fast as if she were battling for the lead in a stakes race. I hadn't asked her; she was running to satisfy her mighty, competitive spirit. She was running for joy.

We came through the second turn. Carmina's head lifted. I sat up, preparing for the worst. "Come on, Carmina, go, girl. Go, go, go!"

She flew past the balking spot with nothing more than a quick ear twitch. "Good girl, oh, you wonderful filly."

We passed under the wire, and still she galloped on. I tightened my hold on the reins, certain she must be tiring, and felt her brace against me. I let her go.

Halfway along the backside she shifted down a gear. I babbled away to her, encouraging her to slow up. The reins were useless in my hands. My own strength was spent; I had just enough energy to keep myself in the saddle. She continued to reduce her stride until finally she was trotting.

Between my ragged gasps for breath I heard her snorting with satisfaction.

Gracefully she gave in to my request for her to walk. My heart was pounding so hard I felt certain I'd have bruises on the inside of my ribs. Carmina didn't protest when I asked her to turn and stop, facing the rail. She pricked her ears, raising her head. I followed her gaze.

On the other side of the track the grooms' stand was packed full.

"Looks like we had an audience, my lady," I said.

Unimpressed, Carmina shook her head and began marching back along the racetrack. I didn't have to direct her to the outside fence; she went there of her own accord. When it came to being a racehorse, this filly knew it all. She'd made one thing clear this morning: she wanted to be *asked* to perform, not told. That huge competitive spirit of hers wouldn't have it any other way.

I had ridden out expecting to teach her a lesson. Instead, she'd taught me one.

Clem caught up to us on Keno. "You did it, Reid. You got her all the way around!"

I didn't even fake modesty. "I did! Pretty amazing, huh? Oh, Clem, she's a great filly, really great."

His eyes were wide and shining with admiration. "You'll get the ride on her in the Lady Perthshire for sure,

Reid. Except for Mom, nobody else could even get her to go around the track!"

"I expect I will," I sighed happily, stroking the filly's damp neck. "I expect I will."

Other horses and riders were coming out on the track. Corky saluted me with his whip. "Good work, Reid."

"Thanks, Corky," I replied.

Walt was less pleased. He grabbed the filly's bridle the moment she stepped off the track. Carmina swung her head, shaking him off like a fly.

"Leave her be, Walt," I said. "I can manage her."

"What in the blue blazes did you think you were doing, taking that filly out there like that?" Walt puffed, scurrying alongside Carmina as she strode back to the barn.

"Training her, Walt. It's this new idea: you take a horse out of the stall and exercise it on the track so it can get fit and run in races." I was cocky with triumph, the smartass words just falling from my mouth.

"You think you're so smart, kid. Do you know what you've done? You've just left that filly's race out there on the racetrack. How could you do something so stupid?" spluttered Walt.

"Her race is six days away. She'll recover."

We turned in to our shed row. I pulled up outside Carmina's stall, kicked my feet free of the stirrups and

77

vaulted off. I ran my stirrup irons up the leathers and undid the girth, pulling off the exercise saddle as Walt struggled to buckle a halter on the filly's tossing head.

"Here, let me." I nudged Walt aside and pushed my saddle into his hands. "Now, sweet lady, be good." Carmina stilled and I fastened her halter. "See, she likes me."

Walt shoved the saddle back at me. "Reid, what are you trying to prove?"

"I'm the best rider for this filly. You have to see that now. She likes me. I'm the only one besides Mom who can get her to go around the racetrack!"

"What I see is a punk kid who thinks he knows it all when he don't know nothing! You think you should get all kinds of breaks just 'cause you're your momma's boy. Well, let me tell you, you've got to prove yourself just like every other pinhead on this track!"

I reached out and tugged Carmina's lead shank away from him. "This is our barn, Walt, not yours. You're not in charge here."

"Oh, don't be so sure about that, boy." Walt stomped away.

"You made him really mad," said Clem from atop Keno. "Now we've got no one to help us with chores and getting the horses out."

I was opening my mouth to tell him to shut up when my

brother jumped off Keno and ran off too, leaving me to do everything on my own. I cranked my jaw shut.

Carmina bunted my shoulder, reminding me she was hot and sweaty. Up and down the shed row, the horses whinnied, demanding to be cared for.

"Good morning!"

Ella Gervais came along the shed row just as the sun broke over the hills, a halo of sunlight behind her.

10.

Ella gave us two hours before she left for her cashier's job. Her help meant we were done by noon, at which time I was starving and ready for a shower and a long siesta. Kicking off my boots outside the trailer, I staggered inside and yanked open the fridge door. Empty, except for a shrivelled lemon, a bottle of ketchup and a chunk of mouldy cheese. I slammed through the cupboards and came up with a few soda crackers and half a box of breakfast cereal.

Clem was right: we needed groceries.

How did Mom do it? I wondered. Feed, clothe and look out for two kids and manage a barn full of racehorses? I knew the answer; I'd realized it a long time ago. It was the reason we were here instead of Woodbine. She'd compromised her career for her family.

I was going to change all that for Mom.

First things first. I had to go shopping, so I needed money. I dug through the cookie tin on top of the fridge and found twenty dollars and some change—and a whole lot of bills.

Overdue bills. With interest owing. One envelope contained the bank statement. I pulled it out and stared at the bottom line. Adding up the bills in my head I quickly realized there wasn't enough in the bank account to cover them.

I set the statement on the table and covered it with my hands. Why hadn't Mom told me we were just about broke?

Now a lot of things made sense. Mom kept "forgetting" to call the farrier, although I reminded her every day. She'd taken to buying a single bag of grain at a time, even though there was a discount for buying ten or more. She'd cancelled our Internet connection, telling us we were spending too much time online and it was free at the public library anyway.

Clement had been outfitted with back-to-school clothes, but that was because Bryant sent his child support every month. I didn't have to check to know Mom wouldn't touch that money for anything else.

The burden of raising me had been one she'd always carried all by herself. Now, finally, it was payback time. The money I'd earned yesterday riding races was waiting for me in the racing office. That, together with Goingmyway's and Marty's winnings, would be enough to buy groceries and get rid of a couple of bills.

I had to get more rides in the next weekend's races, even if it meant getting down on my knees and begging trainers to put me on their horses. But why would they, when the trainer who'd put himself in charge of our barn wouldn't name me on our own horses? I might get a few pity rides out of sympathy for our situation, but until I proved myself, the trainers were going to choose the experienced riders over a newly licensed apprentice. Winning the Lady Perthshire on Carmina wasn't just a matter of getting my riding career off to a quick start anymore. I needed to win so my family could survive.

Mom got out of hospital Wednesday afternoon.

Dressed in her normal clothes—jeans and a T-shirt—with her hair tied back, she looked a hundred times better. Hospital rules said she couldn't walk to the main doors; she had to ride in a wheelchair, which Clem insisted on pushing while giving her a complete moment-by-moment replay of everything that had happened since our last visit. There weren't too many details for me to add in. He didn't miss much, my little brother.

As we crossed the lobby a doctor stopped us.

"Hey there, Tracy. So these must be your sons."

"Yes, they are, Kevin. Reid, Clement, this is Dr. Matthews."

Kevin to her, Dr. Matthews to us? I looked at Mom in surprise. She winked back.

Before I could give the situation too much thought, the doctor shook our hands. "Good to meet you guys. Now, Tracy, remember our talk. You've pushed your luck pretty hard. If there's a next time…well, I think I explained very clearly what the outcome will be." His eyes held Mom's until she looked down. Then he turned to me. "Take care of your mother. She's a very special lady."

"I will," I told him. Dr. Matthews gave me a nod of approval and marched away. "So, what was that all about?"

Mom didn't brush off the doctor's warnings as I expected her to. "We'll talk about it later."

"But—"

"Reid, I'm not up to a long discussion right now. Could we just get out of this place?"

A long discussion about *what*?

I brought the truck around to the entrance. Mom's gait was unsteady as she walked the few steps from the wheel-chair to the truck. I caught her arm. "Hey, are you okay?"

She nodded. "Just a little dizzy, that's all. Please don't fuss, Reid."

"Maybe you should stay in the hospital for a few more days."

"No, I don't want to be stuck in there any longer!"

"All right, all right. It's cool." It was like I was dealing with a small child.

"Don't humour me!" Mom scrambled awkwardly into the truck beside Clem. I shut the door behind her. She reached through the open window and caught my shoulder. "I'm sorry, dear. I'm still a bit over-emotional."

"Don't worry about it, Mom. Everything's cool."

"Will you please stop saying that? It's not cool at all, it's darned hot!" She smiled at her own joke.

I grinned back, relieved to see a trace of my old mom at last. I sprinted around the front of the truck and hopped in the driver's seat. "Okay, let's get this show on the road."

"We're going for ice cream," Clem announced. "Reid's treat. He promised."

I stiffened, waiting for Mom's reaction.

"That's a wonderful idea," she said.

"Where are we going?" asked Clem as I turned onto a side street.

"I thought we'd try this new place." I looked over my shoulder, getting ready to parallel park the truck in front of the ice cream parlour. My elbow pressed the horn, twice, with a short pause between. "Whoops."

I backed the truck into the parking slot and jumped out.

"Hang on a second, Mom, I'll get your door."

"Thank you, Reid." She held my shoulder as she carefully lowered herself to the pavement.

"Hey, there's Ella!" Clem waved at a figure standing at the window of the store next door.

I poked some coins into the parking meter. "Oh, is it?" I said, pretending to be surprised. "I guess that must be where she works."

"Who's Ella?" asked Mom.

"Reid's girlfriend," snickered Clem, ducking away from the expected swat.

"She's a really nice girl who's been helping us out in the mornings," I said, quickly adding "for free" as I remembered the state of our bank account. I held open the door of the ice cream parlour.

Mom and Clem took the cue and went in. My brother's attention was instantly diverted by the wide array of tubs displayed in two long glass cabinets. "I don't know which one to choose! What are you going to have, Mom?"

"Butter pecan. Two scoops, please. In a waffle cone."

"French vanilla for me, please," I said.

"Two scoops?" asked the guy behind the counter. "Waffle cone?"

I shook my head no. "Just one, in a plain cone."

"Come on, Reid, have two scoops," urged Mom.

"No, thanks, just one's enough." I looked at Mom in surprise. She of all people knew how many calories there were in ice cream.

At last, Clem decided on two flavours—a scoop of each.

"Let's stay here where it's nice and cool," I suggested, settling down on a chair at a table in the front of the shop. The other two followed my lead.

The old-fashioned bell over the door tinkled as someone came in.

"Ella! We're over here," called Clem. "Reid, it's Ella."

I turned in my seat, a big grin stretching itself across my face. "Hi, Ella, how's it going?"

"Good, thanks, Reid." She made her way to our table. "Hi, Clement."

"Ella, this is my mom, Tracy. Mom, this is Ella Gervais. She just moved here from up north with her family. She had to leave her horse behind."

"That must have been hard."

"It was," said Ella. Her eyelashes fluttered as she tried not to think about Timber.

"Anyway," I went on, "like I told you, Ella's been giving us a hand in the mornings before she goes in to her other job—mucking out, brushing, tacking up. I don't know what we would have done without her help while you were in the hospital."

Mom smiled up at Ella. "Thank you very much. I really appreciate everything you've done."

Ella's cheeks went pink. "You're very welcome. It's good to be around horses again."

There was a long pause. "Your ice cream's dripping, Reid," Clem pointed out.

I grabbed a napkin and wrapped it around my cone. Mom and Clem licked their cones, their eyes flicking back and forth from me to Ella, who was still standing beside the table. "Would you like to sit down, Ella?"

"Uh, no, Reid. I've got to get back to work."

"But you didn't get any ice cream," said Clem.

"I'll get some after work." She looked at her watch. "My break's just about over."

I took a deep breath. "Mom, I think we should give Ella a job. She's really good with the horses and we're going to need help, with you and me both riding. I figure with Ella helping I can gallop in the mornings for other barns and make a lot more money than I am now."

Mom held up her hand to cut me off. "Hang on, there, Reid. You should have run this plan of yours by me before you brought someone else in."

"I just thought if you met Ella you'd see what a great person she is and how good she'd fit in."

"And I can. It's just that...well, things have changed."

"What do you mean?"

Mom's eyes darted around the small shop as if she was trapped. "This isn't the right time."

"Um, I think I'd better go," said Ella. She was out the door before I had a chance to say anything to her.

Back at the track we sprawled in lawn chairs in the shade of the trailer. There were a hundred things Mom and I needed to talk about, not to mention the long discussion she'd promised at the hospital, but my eyelids, open since the crack of dawn, were suddenly as heavy as lead weights. I let them fall shut, just for a few minutes.

When I woke up, the sun was setting on the hills. Mom and Clem were nowhere to be seen. Over in the barns, horses were yelling. Evening chores were well underway.

I knew I should get up and go to work, but I felt reluctant to leave my comfortable lawn chair. If I didn't move, maybe time would stay still along with me. Mom's big talk, which I sensed wouldn't be anything good, wouldn't happen. Ella would keep on coming in the mornings.

And I'd make the decisions about running our stable, as I'd been doing for the last four days while Mom had been in hospital. I had put in long hours and worked hard, but it had felt good to make my own choices. To be in charge.

I'd done a darned good job, if I did say so myself. The

horses were all healthy, happy and sound. Some of them had even improved under my care, I thought. Carmina was the prime example. Early this morning, ignoring Walt's protests, I'd taken her out again with Clem and Keno. She'd put up a bit of fuss, but not much, and I'd managed to get her to gallop slowly twice around. I'd ridden her as well as Mom. Maybe even better.

I realized I hadn't yet talked to Mom about my successes with Carmina. There'd been too many interruptions and too little privacy. She was right: things *had* changed, and I needed to bring her up to date. I sprang up and jogged through the growing shadows to the barn.

Walt had beaten me to it I discovered when I turned in to the shed row. He paced about in front of Mom as she sat on a plastic chair outside the tack room. Clem dragged a hose down the shed row, going from stall to stall topping up water buckets.

I stood in the shadows for a few moments, watching. Judging from the arm waving and jaw flapping, Walt had a lot to say. Mom sat back and let him ramble on. She rolled her shoulders and pressed her hand to her head.

"Are you okay, Mom?" I asked, joining them.

She shrugged. "A bit of a headache. Walt, can we talk about this tomorrow?"

He scowled. "Entries in the morning, Tracy. You're

going to have to decide soon."

"I know."

"Look, why don't you leave things in my hands for a few more days. You're not up to this right now."

"I'm fine," she said sharply. "I appreciate everything you've done for this stable the last few days and I thank you for it. You've been a very good friend. I know how much time you've had to give up to help out, and I can't ask you to give up any more. It just wouldn't be fair."

"Tracy, I don't mind."

"I know you don't, Walt, but I'm not going to take advantage of your good nature."

"Well, if you're sure you can manage," he said gruffly.

"I am. But if I need some help, you'll be the first person I'll ask."

"You do that. Okay, then, I'm heading for my supper." He gave Mom a quick hug. "Take care of yourself, Tracy. You're like a daughter to me. And you, young Reid," he said, play-punching me lightly on the shoulder, "you're a good boy. Basically." He ruffled my hair and I ducked out of reach.

"He treats me like a little kid," I complained when Walt was out of range.

Mom grinned up at me. "Me too."

11.

Somehow, what with one thing and another, Mom and I didn't get around to doing any serious talking that night. We finished at the barn and went back to the trailer for a cold supper. After we'd cleaned everything up, we settled down outside to enjoy the evening cool.

I'd started to tell her the details of my rides on Carmina, with plenty of help from Clem, when, from all over the campground, people began to drop by, packing chairs and sitting themselves down beside us to welcome Mom home.

The storytelling began, as it always does when race-trackers get together. Past glories were relived in vivid detail, and future triumphs forecast. As the night sky darkened, memories grew bolder, recalling faster horses, smarter trainers, and jockeys with more courage in their veins than red blood. And then there were the yarns about luck, lots and lots of racing luck, most of it going where it wasn't deserved.

There were so many tall tales that needed to be told, and retold, that no one seemed to notice Mom's lack of participation. She was curled in a chair with a blanket tucked around her, smiling and laughing at all the right times, but often when I looked over she was gazing up at the stars. Once she turned her head away from the gathering, pressing a corner of the blanket to each eye. When she turned back, a smile was fixed firmly on her face.

Then the focus of the evening changed to a brand new subject: me. Everyone had something to offer up about everything I'd done while Mom was away. Each race I'd ridden was replayed in great detail, some of which I didn't even remember myself. Of course, my morning gallops on Carmina couldn't be overlooked. The praises of my bravery and skill, brightly coloured with drama, heated up the night. As I basked in the warmth, it took me a while to realize that Carmina was being painted with heavy strokes as a black-hearted, evil-tempered equine villain.

"No, no, she's not like that," I protested. "She's not mean, just…full of herself."

"Is that what you call it?" snorted Randy Sirwah. "Me, I say she's nuts. You wouldn't catch me on that horse."

Sure, Randy, you'd be on her in a flash if you got offered the ride. I kept my thoughts to myself. Still, I couldn't resist giving him a grin to show him he hadn't psyched me out, not at all.

"Doesn't it make you nervous, Tracy, watching your boy on that crazy thing?" Randy persisted.

Like me, Mom said nothing. She understood what Randy was trying to do.

Like me, she knew there was nothing to worry about. Carmina and I had a special bond. Edgy, willful, brave and ambitious, she wasn't an easy horse; the great ones never are. But I had her figured out. She had tested me and found me trustworthy. With my feet in the irons, she would run her very best.

And tomorrow, after I'd worked Carmina, Mom would understand that.

Next morning, with Mom helping, chores were done in no time. She wasn't a hundred percent, moving slowly and resting often, so I wasn't surprised when Corky turned up to ride. I came into the tack room to find him checking out the whiteboard where Mom had written the training schedule for the day.

"What bridle does the red filly go in?" he asked after we'd exchanged good mornings.

There was only one chestnut filly in our barn, but even so, I couldn't believe he meant Carmina. "What red filly?"

"Carmina. Tracy wants me to get in a work on her this morning, before entries open." A work is a timed gallop at racing speed. Usually, almost always, a jockey rides a horse in a work, instead of the exercise rider, because he or she will be named as the rider on that horse for the race.

I lifted Carmina's bridle off its peg. "That's not a good idea."

"Sure it is. A work'll let Tracy know where the filly's at before she puts her in the race. No sense entering her if she's backed up in her training while your mom was off."

"That's not what I mean, Corky. The filly's going real good for me, so *I'd* better ride her in her work." I kept my face blank, though my heart was thumping. Why was I so surprised? Everything that had happened since Mom's accident had warned me this moment would come. I recalled Corky's own words to me: *No one's going to step aside to let you into this game.* Maybe not, but I wasn't going to let anyone push me out of the way, either. I had earned my turn, and I was going to take it.

Corky dragged his hand down his face, pulling the wrinkles smooth. "Come on, Reid, don't make this difficult."

"Why should I make it easy?" I looked him right in the eye.

His eyes held mine without wavering. "Look, this is a tough situation—"

"No, it's not," I cut in. "You're trying to steal my ride, and I'm not going to let you."

"Son, missing the ride in one race is not the end of the world."

"One race, one big race like the Lady Perthshire, could get me on my way. I'm not going to be stuck at this track forever riding a bunch of no-talent nags. I'm going somewhere."

Corky blew out a sigh. "That's what we all thought, once upon a time. You know, Reid, you're a smart boy. You do real good in school. There are lots of ways you can get ahead in this world without doing something as dumb-assed as riding races. You could go to university, get a career."

"Are you telling me you don't think I can make it as a jockey?"

"Don't put words in my mouth, Reid. That's not what I said at all. I'm just pointing out that you've got options. Opportunities I never had."

"Me neither," said Mom from the door. She took the bridle from me and handed it to Corky. He picked up an exercise saddle and left.

"What's going on here? Why the heck is Corky working Carmina and not me?" I demanded.

"Because that's what Mrs. Rogers wants." She avoided my eyes as she said it.

"What does Leona Rogers know? You're the trainer! Tell her I should be on her horse, not Corky."

"Reid, you need to quit acting like a spoiled brat and be mature about this."

"I am being mature! I'm the one who got Carmina around the track after she dumped Corky. Carmina goes better for me than anyone except..."

Finally, I thought to ask the big question. "Mom, why aren't *you* working Carmina?"

She bowed her head, her hands clasped beneath her chin. "I can't. I can't ride anymore."

"Hey, yes, you can. Just get on and go. You won't be afraid once you're on a horse again."

She looked right at me, her eyes shiny with held-in tears. "It's not that. Reid, I've had a lot of concussions. The doctors say one more and I'll have brain damage. Maybe a little, maybe a lot, they can't tell me for sure. If that happened, who would look after you and Clem?"

"That's not going to happen. Not to you."

"I can't take the chance, not with two boys to raise."

"You're going to quit?"

"I have to, Reid. I have no choice." She swiped at her eyes with the heel of her hand.

Now I knew what had been bothering her since she got out of the hospital.

"I'm sorry, Mom." And I was. But even in the middle of feeling bad for my mother, a little voice inside me yelled, *My turn! My turn!* I tried to ignore it and think of something to say that would help pick up her spirits. Clumsily, I patted her shoulder. "Don't worry, we'll make it through this. We'll figure something out."

She squeezed my hand and smiled. "I know we will. We've been through tough times before. Everything will work out for the best. Maybe it's time for a change, time to try something completely different."

"You can get your trainer's licence now. With me riding and you training full-time, we can take more owners. We can move to a bigger track where there's more purse money."

"We'll talk about this later, okay? Right now I need you to go out on the pony with Carmina." Seeing the look on my face, she begged, "Please, Reid. Help me out here."

Everything inside me rose up against what she was asking, but what choice did I really have? If Mom couldn't ride, who else was there but me? Shaking my head in disgust, I pulled on my flak jacket and slammed my helmet onto my head.

"You knew that Mom was quitting, didn't you?" I asked

Corky as we stepped out on the track.

"She didn't say anything to me, if that's what you're asking, but I kind of figured things might go that way. Tracy's taken a lot of hard spills over the years; comes a time when the body just says no more." He chirped Carmina into a jog.

I booted Keno up alongside. "Except for you. Looks like you're going to go forever."

"I should've given it up a long time ago, according to the doctors, except what else is a stupid jock like me going to do? It's not like there's a big fat pension waiting for me when I retire."

"You could be a trainer."

Corky snorted. "Don't know a thing about it. All right now, young lady, let's have none of this."

Carmina's head came up, her gait a mincing prance. Corky's whip stayed in his back pocket. He pulled on one rein and then the other, zigzagging the filly back and forth across the track. She gave up much sooner this time, her ears coming forward and her stride lengthening. "Good for you, Reid, you got her figured out," Corky called to me.

"I didn't do it for you," I muttered.

We were loping now. Carmina's strides were building, longer, stronger, pulling her away from Keno. I let her go, checking over my shoulder for oncoming horse traffic before trotting Keno to the outside of the track. We parked and watched our filly go. A small, mean part of me wanted her to act up, maybe even dump Corky on the track again. But Carmina was all business, aware somehow that there was a big race coming up and the time for goofing off was over.

Coming out of the turn, Corky dropped her down onto the rail. She hit the quarter pole flying, her long legs reaching out and snapping back, her red tail flaming out behind her. Going into the turn, she picked up another worker. Side by side the two horses galloped until Carmina stretched out her giant frame, her stride reaching out for even more ground. She pulled ahead of the other horse like it was slowing down. I could tell by the blur of her churning legs that she was moving faster now than at the beginning of her work.

Corky braced his feet against the stirrups, his hands locked on the reins. Carmina braced her neck and ran right through his stranglehold, going as fast as she pleased. I hustled Keno out onto the track. Corky was up in his stirrups, using his entire body as leverage to slow the filly. I got Keno loping. Carmina bore down on us like a train. Keno opened up and I reached over and hooked onto her reins. My left foot came out of the stirrup but I held firm, trusting my pony to keep a true path.

Even with two people and another horse acting as

ballast, Carmina managed to drag us into the turn before reducing her speed. She was in no hurry to pull up, loping around the turn and into the backstretch before breaking to trot. She was blowing hard, her nostrils flared like trumpets, but she held her head high, her dark eyes bright, while the rest of us, Corky, Keno and I, gasped for air.

The outrider slid to a stop beside us. "You guys okay?"

Corky nodded, waving him away.

We faced the infield, taking a few more moments to catch our breath, before turning around and following the outside rail off the track. Mom met us at the gap, a stopwatch tucked into the palm of her hand. Her face was carefully blank, revealing nothing. She caught Carmina by the bridle. "Fifty-nine and change," she told us, low voiced.

Corky whistled. He patted the filly's neck. "She had lots left in the tank at the end. Look, she's hardly blowing."

But she was. The galloping I'd done with Carmina Monday had been a hobby-horse canter compared to the speed she'd just shown. She was tired, maybe too tired to recover in time for the race.

Ella was at the barn with Clem when we got back. Her cheerful greeting was a welcome break from all the heavy stuff that had been going down. "I woke up early and thought I'd come and see if you guys needed any help. I've got a couple of hours before I have to go to work."

Mom called a greeting to her while I put Keno in his stall and helped Corky pull Carmina's tack and buckle on her halter.

"Gracie next, Reid," Mom said. "Corky, you can take Homer. Clem, help Corky tack him up, please."

"I can do it," offered Ella.

"No, you come with me, Ella." Mom took Carmina and led her to the wash rack.

By the time we had the horses ready, Ella was leading a bathed Carmina around the shed row to cool her out.

"Ella's going to work here a couple of hours in the mornings and on weekends," Mom said, legging me up on Gracie.

"Thanks, Mom," I said.

"I like her. She's a good hand with horses. She gets along really good with Clement, too."

With the extra help the morning went quickly. By the time entries opened, Corky had left and we were cooling out the last horses.

"I'm heading over to the office," said Mom.

"Mom! Wait up!" I pushed Marty's lead shank into Clem's hands and ran after her. "Who are you putting up on Carmina?"

Her eyes told me the answer right away. "Honey, I have no choice."

"Yes, you do! Carmina goes better for me than anyone else! You saw what happened this morning—she ran off with Corky. He couldn't hold her; he's not strong enough anymore. He's too old."

"Reid, it's not just my decision. Mrs. Rogers wants Corky on her filly."

"What does she know? You're the trainer! Tell her I'm the better rider for her horse. Because it's true, Mom, I am."

Mom looked away.

And then I knew. Even my own mother wasn't going to give me a chance. "You're making a big mistake here," I told her and stormed off.

My gut was churning hard, threatening to puke. I needed to get away from everyone before I either threw up or blew up, maybe both. As I stomped past the shed row, Ella called out to me. "Reid, Clem needs help."

Marty was towing my little brother. I grabbed the shank and gave it a snap to get the horse's attention. Instantly he found his manners again.

Ella recoiled at the scowl twisting my face. "What's wrong?"

"Nothing," I snarled.

"I think I know," said Clem in a whisper so loud I had no trouble hearing it.

"Be quiet, Clem."

I might as well have told the birds to hush. He hurried to Ella's side to relay the whole sorry situation. I picked up my pace, hurrying Marty out of earshot. It was nothing I needed to hear about all over again.

By the time the horses were dry I'd settled down enough to offer Ella a ride to work.

She hesitated, studying my face. I made an effort and smoothed out the frown lines on my forehead. She nodded. "All right."

She'd ridden her bike to the track. I lifted it into the truck, and we got in the cab. I jammed the truck into gear and roared out of the parking lot onto the street.

"Reid, pull over and let me out!"

"What?"

"If you're going to drive like an idiot, I want out!"

I slowed down. "I'm sorry. Things are just real crappy in my life right now."

"Yes, well, getting into an accident would only make things worse. Clem told me some of the stuff that's happened. Do you want to talk about it?"

"What good is talking going to do?"

"Maybe no good at all. Or maybe it'll help you see things in a different way."

"What did Clem tell you?"

"That your mom's not going to be a jockey anymore

and Corky's going to ride Carmina in that big race, I can't remember the name of it."

"The Lady Perthshire Stakes. How does Clem know about all of this? I just found out."

"He eavesdrops. He hides under windows and outside doors so he can listen in. I told him that was sneaky, but he said he has to because no one ever tells him anything about what's going on."

"Well, he's not the only one who gets kept in the dark," I grumbled.

"Reid, I know this race is worth a lot of money, but there'll be other races for you to ride in, won't there?"

"Sure, there'll be other races, lots and lots of races, most of them on second-rate horses that barely run fast enough to spread their own manure. It's the ride on Carmina that's important, Ella. Horses with her talent hardly ever end up at this level. I could wait a long time before I get a chance like this again. It's fate, don't you see?"

"I guess so. What you're telling me is Carmina is going to win the Lady Perthshire and whoever's riding her will be a hero."

"That's about it." I pulled up to a stop sign at the end of the street.

"And that rider will be Corky Sinclair."

"That's who Leona Rogers wants on her horse. But she's

never watched me ride Carmina. She's never seen how much better the filly goes for me."

"So tell her. There she is right now." She pointed out the window. Sure enough, there was Leona Rogers going into the coffee shop on the corner. "Go on, Reid. Give it a try."

"But I have to get you to work."

"I've got my bike. I can ride the rest of the way."

Before I'd even thought through what I was doing, I'd turned in to a parking lot. Ella hopped out and hauled out her bike before I'd pulled the key from the ignition.

"Hey, Reid," she said, "why don't you come for supper tonight at my place?" When I didn't answer right away, she tipped her head to one side, those caramel-brown eyes soft and pleading. "Please?"

How could I say no? "Sure. That'd be nice. What time?"

"After you're done chores. Don't worry, we won't keep you up late. Mom and Dad have to leave for work before eight. Well, see you tonight." She swung her leg over her bike and pedalled away. "Good luck!"

"Thanks, I'll need it," I muttered to myself. Jamming the key in my pocket, I crossed the parking lot.

I was so busy inside my own head I didn't notice the man holding the door open for me until he spoke. "Reid, done at the track already?" asked Walt Fletcher.

"Huh? Oh, hi, Walt." I scooted by, passing on his question. Hopefully, he was grabbing a coffee to go. I thought I'd head for the men's room to avoid him; then Leona Rogers looked up and waved me over. I made my way to her corner table, wishing Walt wasn't there. "Good morning, Mrs. Rogers."

"Oh, hello, Reid. Goodness, what a surprise to see you here!" She looked around me, waved again to someone else.

"Mrs. Rogers, can I talk to you about something?"

"Of course you can. Please, sit down."

I'd just settled into the chair opposite when Walt dropped into the seat beside Mrs. Rogers. "Morning, Leona. You look lovely today, hon." He slung his arm around her shoulders and squeezed.

"Thank you, Walt." She preened, fluttering her eyelashes. Their eyes held, long enough that I began to think they'd forgotten I was there.

I realized Mrs. Rogers hadn't been waving to me at all but to the man behind me: Walt. My face warmed and I felt like an idiot. My chair scraped against the floor as I pushed it back, getting ready to escape, and they both turned to look at me.

"So, Reid, what can we do for you?" Walt's bushy brows lifted to his hairline in frank curiosity.

"My business is with Mrs. Rogers."

The eyebrows twitched even higher. He gestured for me

to speak.

"This is a private conversation, Walt," I told him.

"Well, now, Reid, anything you need to say to Leona you can say to me." He held up Mrs. Rogers' left hand to display a diamond ring. "Leona has done me the honour of accepting my proposal. We're going to be married."

Leona Rogers beamed at him and then me. "You're the first person we've told today, Reid. Walt proposed just last night."

Walt laughed openly at my shock. "Close your mouth, son, you're not at the dentist."

I cranked my jaw shut. Now a lot of things made sense: Mrs. Rogers' unusual visit to the track, Walt's possessiveness over Carmina.

Carmina! Did this mean Walt would be her trainer now? The question fell out of my mouth.

"Heavens, no," said Leona, not even glancing at Walt. I was relieved to see she wasn't entirely under his thumb. "That wouldn't be fair to Tracy."

Walt nodded. "We won't be making any changes so close to the big race. We'll see how Carmina comes out of the race and take it from there."

"Now, Reid"—Mrs. Rogers laid her hands on the table, ring finger on top—"what did you want to talk about with us, dear?"

I shook my head. "It doesn't matter anymore."

"Come on, Reid, have your say," said Walt.

I was sure I could feel Ella poking me in the shoulder. I had a choice: make an idiot of myself right now or wait until later when I went to Ella's for supper. I quickly decided the first option would be the least painful.

"I want you to put me on Carmina in the Lady Perthshire," I blurted out.

"Not this again," groaned Walt. Leona shushed him.

I took a long breath and plowed on. "Carmina and I, we understand each other. She likes me. She'll try harder for me than anyone else, except my mom. I know you think I'm inexperienced and unproven, but I'm not really. I've been around the track all my life. I've watched races since I was in diapers. I—"

Leona reached over the table to lay her hands on mine. "Reid, I appreciate all the hard work you've put into my filly." She gave a little squeeze. "But I don't pick the jockey for my horse; my trainer does."

"But you pay the bills. You have some say in who rides your horse."

"I trust my trainer's judgment, and she's chosen Corky Sinclair. I'm sorry, Reid, but I can't interfere." She darted a quick look at Walt, who was studying his fingernails. "You know, you and Tracy need to do some talking."

My eyes rolled before I could stop them. I caught Walt watching me with a funny look—sympathy?

It was time to leave. I'd done everything I could here. I stood up.

Leona had more to say. "Remember, when one door closes, another one opens, Reid. Life is full of opportunities, especially for a young person like you. Keep your options open, okay?"

I thanked them both for their time, remembered a congratulation and beat a hasty retreat before any more life advice was handed out. Then I got in the truck and banged my head against the steering wheel.

Keep your options open, Leona Rogers had said. How was I going to do that when every single person who could help me slammed the door in my face?

12.

I found my mother in a chair in front of the tack room. There was a tangle of bridles at her feet and a small sponge and a bar of saddle soap beside her, but she had her eyes shut, her face tipped back to the late morning sun. I stood in front of her. "I want to talk to you."

Her eyes blinked open. "Reid. I must have dozed off. What do you want, son?"

"I just talked with Leona Rogers. She says it was your decision to ride Corky and not me on Carmina. Is that the truth?"

"You saw Leona? Here at the track?"

I shook my head impatiently. "I met up with her when I drove Ella to work. She was at a coffee shop. With Walt. They're going to get married."

Mom nodded her head, not at all surprised by the news. "Have they picked the date?"

"You already knew about this?"

"They stopped in to tell me last night." She leaned down to scoop up a bridle.

"Last night? When? Where was I?"

"You were already in bed. It was quite late." Rubbing saddle soap into that bridle was taking a lot of her attention.

"I didn't hear anyone come to the trailer."

"Walt called me on my cell and asked me to come to the tack room. He was there with Leona and they told me."

"They know you have to get up early. Why didn't they just wait until morning?"

She shrugged. "I guess they just had to share the good news with someone."

"Mom, there's more, isn't there? Tell me."

She looked up at me, her eyes squinting against the sun. "Sit down, Reid, so I can see you properly."

"Just tell me, will you!"

"Don't you talk to me like that, young man."

"Sorry," I muttered. Stifling an impatient sigh, I turned over a bucket and sat down with my face forced into what I hoped was a pleasant expression. *What's going on?* I silently demanded.

"Leona and Walt want to do some travelling after they're married. Leona's not ready to sell the farm, but she wants the freedom to come and go. So she's decided to get a live-in caretaker. She's putting in a brand new mobile home—real nice, three bedrooms, skylights; she showed me pictures of it."

She glanced over at me like she was checking out my reaction.

"Sounds great," I said, wishing she'd get to the point.

"You know, Reid, while I was in hospital I did a lot of thinking. About choices I've made. Things I could have done differently. I realized that every step I've taken in my life has gone down a road that's gotten narrower and narrower until now I'm in a place where I can barely turn around."

"What are you saying? That you don't have a good life?"

"No, no, not at all. I have a great life. I've got my wonderful boys and good friends. But I could have had all this in another life, too. What I'm trying to tell you is that I threw away a lot of choices, didn't even give them a second look, and now I have very few left. I don't want that for you or Clem. So when Leona and Walt asked me if I'd go live on the farm as the caretaker, it seemed like a heaven-sent opportunity."

My brain stalled at this point. I sat there on that bucket,

blinking hard to get it working again. "You mean you're going to leave the track?"

She nodded. "It's a beautiful farm. Close to town, too, so you and Clem won't have far to go to school. You'll be able to have friends over. The work's not much, mostly looking after her old horses and taking care of the house, and they're giving me a wage, too. We've got full run of the farm, so if we want to take in some lay-ups from the track or break a few horses to make some extra money, we're welcome to. There's a river you kids can swim in and a couple of dogs. You've always wanted a dog."

"But what about training the horses? Where would we do that?"

She scooped up another bridle from the pile at her feet, working the thin leather straps in her hands. "Well, that's the thing, Reid. We wouldn't be running horses anymore."

"You mean we'd give up racing?"

"It's good to try out different things. Life is short; you don't want to get yourself stuck doing the same things year after year just because you don't know what else is out there."

"Whoa! Mom, stop!" I held up my hands. "Just stop! You can't change our plan, not now."

"What are you talking about, Reid? What plan?"

"Mom, you know, *The* Plan." She looked confused so I

laid it out for her, reminding myself she was still recovering from a concussion and not thinking straight. "You've been teaching me for years so I can take over the race riding when you quit. You'll take out your licence and train full-time, and I'll ride for you. We agreed on this years ago."

"Oh, Reid, that was just a daydream. Things have changed."

"No, they haven't, not for me!"

"Reid, I want you to take a good look around you at the place we're in right now. See that fence that runs all the way around us?"

"Of course I do. It's always been there. This is a race-track; it has to be fenced in case a horse gets loose."

"And it shuts out the rest of the world! We're stuck here in our own little world, cut off from everyone else on this planet."

"So what? It's a good world."

"You don't know any other kind of life."

"I don't need to. Mom, why have you gone all weird like this?"

"My head has never been so clear. I see now that I shouldn't have encouraged you to follow in my footsteps."

"I want to be a jockey! More than anything else in the world."

"That's because you don't know what else you can be.

Reid, you have so many choices. You want to keep your mind open, try a bit of everything the world has to offer you."

"This is why you put Corky on Carmina instead of me—to give me more choices?"

"I want you to know you can be more than just a jockey, that you don't have to end up like me with no money, no education and a broken body."

"You're taking away my chance to ride the best horse we've ever had just to teach me a lesson?"

"No, that's not what I'm doing at all. Carmina's a tough ride—she blows up on post parade, she's difficult in the gate and she's hard to rate."

"So you think an old man can handle her better than me? Thanks, Mom, for finally letting me know what a lousy rider you think I am."

"Reid, you know that's not true. I just don't want anything to happen to you."

"You mean you're scared I'll get hurt?"

"Yes! Yes, I am. You're young, you've got your whole life ahead of you. One split second and all that could change... forever."

"Mom, *nothing's* going to happen."

"You don't know that! This is the most dangerous professional sport there is. More jockeys are killed each year than people in any other sport."

"People are killed every *day* in car accidents—maybe I should never get in a car again, either. Come on, Mom, get a grip. You'll go crazy thinking like this."

She was quiet for a long time. I tugged a loose thread on the hem of my jeans, hoping she was getting ready to change her mind.

"All right, here's the deal," she said at last. "Wait two years, until you're eighteen and finished school. If you still want to be a jockey then, I'll give you my full support."

My head was shaking before she was done talking. "No. No way. I'm not quitting."

"I'm not asking you to quit, just put things on hold for a couple of years."

"I'm not going to quit, and I'm not going to wait for two years. Now, are you going to put me on Carmina? Tell me right now you're going to do it. *Please.*"

She pressed her lips together and said nothing.

I stood up.

"Then I'm out of here."

I went past her into the tack room, snatching up my helmet, flak jacket, boots and exercise saddle. A sheet of paper fluttered to the floor. I grabbed it, checked the date and stuffed it in my helmet.

"Reid, what are you doing?" Mom followed me in.

"Leaving."

"Now just calm down. You don't want to do this."

"I am calm, and yes, I do. It's time to cut the apron strings, Mom. I'm not your little boy anymore."

"Okay, you're upset, I get it. And you're right, I should have talked about this with you before—"

"This is not about discussing your decisions. This is about me making my own. You know, you go on and on about all these choices I'm supposed to have, but did you let me make my own? No, you chose for me, just like you've always done. Well, this is my life, and I'm going to live it my way." I shouldered past her out the door.

At the trailer, Clem was lying in the shade reading a library book. He followed me inside. "What are you doing?"

I dug a duffle bag out from under my bunk and tossed my gear in it. Jeans, shirts and underwear followed. "Leaving."

"What do you mean?"

"I mean I'm leaving. Going away. Getting out." No sense taking my dirty clothes. Pulling our cell phone out of my pocket, I handed it to Clem and changed my jeans and shirt for clean ones.

"You're running away from home? Does Mom know?"

I zipped the bag. "Oh, she knows all right."

"Where are you going?"

"I don't know. Somewhere. Anywhere but here." I

hugged him hard. "Take care of things here, okay, Clem?"

"Reid, don't go! Come back. Please, Reid." He was crying.

I slung the duffle bag over my shoulder and walked out the door.

I followed the side road into the city, wandering up and down a few streets before crashing in a park under a shady tree. Clem's question had been a good one: where *was* I going? I had no answer, just an iron certainty I wouldn't be turning around and heading back to my mother's barn.

I felt like crap about leaving my little brother crying, but what was I supposed to do? Sooner or later I was going to have to go out on my own, and now I had no choice but to go for the sooner option.

My belly was grumbling about food, but I was used to that. I could miss lunch and not be too bothered. Then I remembered Ella's invitation to supper. As much as I hated to disappoint her, I knew I had to cancel. In this mood I wasn't fit to be around civilized people, especially her parents. I'd find a pay phone and tell her I wouldn't be coming.

But not right now. Too much had happened too quickly. I needed some time to let things settle in my head.

Outside my oasis of cool shade, the day was heating up. Wisps of cloud marbled the blue sky. I tucked my duffle bag under my head, stretched out and fell asleep.

I woke up feeling a lot of time had passed. I had no watch and couldn't be sure exactly how much, but the sun was a lot closer to the hilltops. I lay on my back watching the clouds thickening above me, enjoying the luxury of wasting time. My stomach rumbled, and I remembered I had to contact Ella. I picked up my bag and began walking toward the commercial district in search of a pay phone.

When I finally found one, I was only a few blocks from her store. I paused for a moment and kept on walking.

I didn't let myself think too hard about what I was doing next, just let my feet carry me along the sidewalks until I stood in front of the More for Less. I finger-combed my hair and checked my shirt was tucked in, then followed a mother herding three kids through the door. I just wanted to see Ella, the one person who tried to see things from my side of the fence. My plans for the future were sketchy, but I was sure they didn't involve hanging around this town much longer. I needed to make money and find a place to stay. The only way I knew of getting both was to head to another racetrack and get work galloping horses in the morning and a tack room to sleep in. I hadn't decided on which track. Probably I would walk over to the bus station and let the schedule choose my direction for me.

My fledgling jockey career would suffer. I hadn't built

any kind of reputation yet that I could carry with me to another track. But I wasn't going to get anywhere staying here with my mother blocking my way. No, the best thing would be to start somewhere new. I'd have to spend a lot of time pestering trainers to put me up on their horses in the afternoon, but eventually, sooner or later, someone would ride me in a race. I knew I could make one chance lead into a whole bunch more.

Until this moment I hadn't realized my brain had gone ahead and sorted things out for me. It had instructed my feet to bring me here, and now, spotting Ella stacking a shelf with cans of tomato sauce, I understood why. I couldn't just go out of her life, leaving her with a bunch of questions that would never get answers. I had to tell her goodbye.

Someone approached me. "Hey, kid, you've got to leave that bag with our personnel at the front checkout." A badge over the man's shirt pocket said *Store Manager*.

Hearing his voice, Ella looked up. "Reid!" A smile spread over her face.

"I just have to talk to her for a second."

The manager shook his head. "No backpacks in the store. No exceptions. Either take it to the counter, or I'll have to escort you from the store."

No wonder Ella wanted a different job. The guy was

an idiot. I looked in his eyes and saw that he was enjoying this, pushing around someone smaller. He wasn't really old, maybe close to thirty, but already his belly was bulging out over his belt. I kept my gaze steady, and he began to shift from foot to foot.

"Go on, get out of here!" There was definitely a squeak in his voice now.

"Hey, stay chill, man, I'm going." Behind his shoulder Ella held up ten fingers. I nodded and swung suddenly around. The manager grunted as my bag hit his belly. "Whoops, sorry, didn't know you were so close."

"Go on, get out of here!"

I did.

A blanket of clouds had been pulled across the sky, blocking out the sun and weighing down the air. I sat on the steps of a neighbouring business, returning the stares of the homeless guy on the other side of the street, and waited.

Ella came and silently sat down beside me. I opened my arms and pulled her close.

She took me home. I don't know what she told her parents in the living room while I stood just inside the back door, but it didn't take long for her mother to offer me a bed for the night.

Mrs. Gervais sprang into action in the kitchen, fixing

an early supper, while Ella's father showed me to her little brother Simon's room, where I was given the bottom bunk bed, and then the bathroom so I could wash up. Leading the way down the hall between the two rooms, he turned around and fixed me with a stern look.

"My wife and I will be at work tonight. I expect you to treat my daughter with nothing less than total respect. Do you understand what I'm saying, Reid?"

"I do, sir. Absolutely." My head was nodding like a bobble-head doll. "I will. Completely."

"Good. My younger daughter and son will be here too, and if I hear otherwise…" His eyes narrowed to slits.

"You won't, sir. I promise you." I found myself holding up my palm, like I was swearing an oath.

His hand clapped down on my shoulder. "Call me Doug. And my wife's name is Rita. Clean up and come have something to eat."

"Thank you. Doug. Thanks for letting me stay."

"You're very welcome, Reid."

The whole family and I sat down to a meal of cold chicken, buns and salads outside at a table on a small cement-block patio. The sky was completely overcast now, the temperature easing a few degrees. We held hands, and Mr. Gervais—Doug—said the grace before we began. I sat between

Simon, a stocky boy about thirteen who was already taller than me, and Louisa, who was nearly ten and giggled whenever I looked at her. Ella was beside her mother.

Simon and Louisa kept glancing at me but didn't ask questions. The food was great, all of it homemade. Mom and I hardly ever had time to cook, so I was used to eating a lot of convenience foods.

"Where are you putting it all, son?" asked Doug Gervais as I took second helpings of everything. "I thought jockeys had to watch their weight."

"Mostly we do. I don't usually eat like this, but everything's so good. Mrs. Gervais, you are a wonderful cook."

"Reid, please, call me Rita. Surely you don't have weight problems. You're as skinny as a rail."

"I do 120, or 125 if I let myself go. My apprentice allowance lets me ride at 115, so that means losing about five pounds before I ride."

"How do you do that?" asked Simon.

I shrugged. "There's ways. Exercising, sweating, fasting."

Rita Gervais looked over at her husband with an alarmed expression. "But you're so young. How can you do that to your body? It can't be healthy."

"I have to, if I want to ride races." If this was their reaction to the realities of a jockey's life, I was happy I hadn't given them the whole list of jockeys' quick weight-loss methods.

Doug pushed his plate aside and propped his elbows on the table. "Tell me something, Reid: from what I understand, being a jockey isn't a long-term career. How old will you be when you retire?"

"I don't know." I'd been working hard at getting my career going, not worrying about retirement. "All depends. Some riders quit in their thirties; others keep going forever. Look at Corky Sinclair, he's fifty-six years old. Usually it's the weight that gets you, not age. You get older and it starts packing on and won't come off."

"It's a very dangerous profession, isn't it?" asked Rita. "Wasn't your mother badly hurt recently?"

"Yes, she was. She's going to be okay, but she's not going to ride anymore."

"I'm glad to hear that. It must be so hard for her to watch you ride in horse races."

I shrugged my reply. Maybe that was what was bothering Mom: watching me beginning my career while hers was ending, and not through her own choice. Though somehow that just didn't seem like my mother, who'd always been so generous with her encouragement and instruction. Still, it was a big change.

"I'd be worried to bits if you were my son," Rita went

on, "and I'm sure it's worse for your mother because she knows first-hand the dangers and risks you're facing."

I shook my head. "Mom doesn't worry." I didn't mean to lie, but I had to do something to resist all the fear that was floating around like a virus. I couldn't let it infect me. "She knows nothing like that's going to happen to me."

"*All* mothers worry about their children, Reid. Every single one of us. It's part of our job description." She stood up and began gathering the dirty plates.

"Not my mom. She's a jockey. And now she's a trainer."

"Really? Then why do you call her Mom?"

"Because…she's my mother."

"That's right. You don't call her Jockey or Trainer. You call her Mom, because that's what she is. Before anything else, she's your mother."

They left for work soon after, preparing to clean offices all night long. Mrs. Gervais hugged her kids and me good-bye while Doug issued mock military orders for us to do the dishes, tidy the house and behave. He turned to me last of all, eyebrows raised. I nodded: *Yes, sir!*

After we'd cleaned everything up, Simon and Louisa went to hang out with friends in the neighbourhood. I sat on the back steps with Ella, watching with unseeing eyes as purple-bellied clouds massed overhead. Without chores, the evening felt strangely unfinished. I wondered how the horses were doing. Then I found myself missing Clem, of all people, and wondering what he was doing. I could hear Louisa and her friends shrieking and laughing as they played freeze-tag nearby, and I wished Clem was there to play too. There weren't many kids at the campground right now, and he was the youngest by far.

"Sorry about Mom," said Ella, breaking the silence. "She fusses about stuff."

"She's a nice lady. Your parents are good people."

"They're pretty decent for parents," she agreed.

"So...what did you tell them?"

"About why you needed a place to stay? Not much. I just said you and your mother weren't getting along and were taking a time-out, so you needed a place to sleep for a few nights."

"That's all? They didn't want to know more?"

"Nope. People have stayed with us before. Mom comes from a big family, and both her sister and her cousin lived with us for a while when they were having problems at home. So we're used to it."

"Wow. That's amazing."

"You think so? It just seems normal to me. I think your family's amazing." She propped her elbows on her knees and cupped her chin in her hands. "What happened, Reid? Why did you leave?"

A lump had risen in my throat, put there by the kindness of these people who had taken me in and fed me without question. "I'll be right back," I said hoarsely.

In Simon's room, I pulled the folded piece of paper from my helmet and took it back outside to Ella.

"What is this?"

"The overnight. It's a list of the horses entered in Sunday's races along with their trainers and possible jockeys."

Her eyes scanned down the list line by line. "Oh, look, there you are!"

"Where?" I leaned over her shoulder. She pointed to a horse in the second race. Sure enough, I'd been named as the rider on a horse named Country Magic.

"And you're on the two horse in the fourth race. Did I say that right—the two horse?"

"Yes, you did. Who's the horse?"

"You mean you don't know?"

"I haven't actually looked at the overnight until now. The jockeys aren't always told about the trainers' plans in advance, especially for minor races."

She passed the list back to me, then ran her finger down the page and stopped next to my name. I was on a decent horse with a good trainer. We were in with a chance.

Ella's finger continued down the page, slowing at the last race. Finding Carmina's name, it traced across the page until it was under Corky Sinclair's name. "So Mrs. Rogers wouldn't change her mind." She sounded nearly as disappointed as I felt.

"She said the choice of jockey was her trainer's decision."

"Walt Fletcher?"

"No. My mom. That's why I left, Ella. We had a fight and I finally learned the truth: she doesn't think I'm going to cut it as a jockey." I bowed my head. A drop of rain hit the back of my neck. "She told me to look into a different line of work."

"Reid, did she really say that?"

"Not in those exact words, but it's sure as heck what she meant."

"But she's so proud of you. You can hear it in her voice every time she talks about you. It doesn't make any sense."

"No, it doesn't," I agreed. "But the fact remains: Corky's on Carmina and not me."

"Give me that!" Ella snatched away the overnight as I began to crumple it in my hands. She turned sideways, smoothing it on the stair beside her.

I buried my head in my hands.

"Reid." Ella poked my ribs. "What does 'no rider' mean?"

"There's no jockey named to the horse yet."

She jabbed me again. "Look! This horse—Eve's

Dream—needs a rider. In the Lady Perthshire. She's trained by Roy Laughlin."

"Never heard of the guy."

"So what? Get hold of him, Reid. Tell him you want to ride his horse."

"What for? She'll never beat Carmina."

"Oh, come on, Reid, stop whining."

"She's probably a dog with no chance of winning. That's why no one wants the ride on her."

"But anything can happen in a horse race! Go see this trainer. Say you'll do it!" She dug her elbow in my side.

"Hey, that hurt!" I sat up.

"I thought jockeys were supposed to be real tough."

"We are. I am." I rubbed my rib cage. "But that still hurt."

"Want me to kiss it better?" She tipped her head to one side.

"Hmm, that might help. But this would be a lot better." I reached out and cupped my hand around her face to draw her close. Her skin was as soft as petals. I pressed my lips to hers, and suddenly the world was spinning over and around until I didn't know which way was up. I was sinking, drowning in the sweet spice of her scent, her warmth, the firm touch of her arms wrapped around me, her hands clasping my back.

"You guys know you're getting all wet?"

Ella pulled away. Simon stood just inside the screen door, Louisa giggling beside him. "Have you been spying on us?" Ella demanded furiously.

"Uh-huh. Dad told me to keep an eye on you two."

I swore softly under my breath.

"We weren't doing anything wrong, Simon Gervais, so you keep your big mouth shut, you hear me?"

I got to my feet and reached out a hand to Ella to help her up. The rain was serious now, and we were both well on the way to being soaked. We went inside, Ella pushing past her brother and stomping off to her room. Simon came with me to his room. "Listen, Reid, about my sister—"

"Hey, it was just a kiss. No big deal." That didn't sound right. "What I mean is, I really like Ella. She's a wonderful girl, and I wouldn't do anything to hurt her." I pulled dry clothes from my bag. "Do you think I could have a shower?"

Simon stepped in front of me. "You treat Ella good. Understand?" He poked his finger in my chest to drive his point home.

I grabbed his hand and held it. He was a bit taller than me and heavier, but he had the soft muscles of a computer geek. "I wouldn't treat her any other way. Do you understand?"

He nodded. I let him yank his hand away. "Okay, then. Sure, go ahead and grab a shower, but you're going to have to wait. Ella's already beat you to it. Let's hope she doesn't use all the hot water."

"Yes, let's hope."

Imitating his father, he clapped me on the shoulder.

I pretended to stagger. "Hey, take it easy there, guy."

His chuckles followed me down the hall into the living room, where we sat slack jawed and blank faced in front of the television until Ella was finally out of the bathroom.

About four minutes into my shower, the hot water ran out.

13.

Daybreak the next morning found me back at the place I'd left less than twenty-four hours before. Ella was by my side. She'd offered to quit working for Mom, to show her support for me, but I knew by the look in her eyes she didn't really want to. In the end, we'd agreed it would be childish and irresponsible to leave Mom even more short-handed, so Ella headed straight to Mom's barn to help with morning chores.

Walking through the backstretch on my own, I ignored the curious looks and dodged all the questions by pretending to be blind and hard of hearing. Popping into the kitchen I got the information I needed and made my way to Roy Laughlin's barn, to find an old couple puttering through their morning chores of feeding and mucking out the stall of their lone racehorse. Oh, and her nineteen-year-old companion, a very fat light grey—named Snowball, of course. I learned that from the handmade sign tacked onto his door.

"Morning! I'm looking for Roy."

"That would be me. This is my good wife, Evie. What can I do for you, young fella?" He shook my hand with a surprisingly strong grip.

"I'm Reid Widmark. I understand you need a rider for your horse on Sunday."

"Might or might not. You offering your services?"

"Yes, sir, I am."

He sucked in his cheeks and eyed me up and down. "You're just a kid. What makes you think you're good enough for my horse?"

That was ridiculous. Roy Laughlin should have been falling all over any rider willing to get aboard his unknown horse. "I could tell you all kinds of stories about what a great rider I am, but you'll find that out for yourself if you put me on your horse," I told him.

Roy Laughlin said nothing back to that for a long time. He rubbed his chin and stared at the toes of his boots. I shuffled my feet, getting ready to leave once he found the words to turn me down. Truthfully, I was a bit relieved. I could tell this was a low-budget mom-and-pop operation, and I didn't expect their horse to amount to much. The whole point of riding in the Lady Perthshire was to make a name for myself by coming under the wire first. Running up the racetrack with the rest of the losers wouldn't do too much to help along my budding career as a jockey.

"Come over here, Reid." Roy lowered himself under the chain of his filly's stall and motioned to me to follow him inside. "What do you make of this horse?"

I hesitated, wondering just how much honesty he wanted.

"Go on, say what you need to."

I slid my hand down the dark bay's neck, feeling the well-toned muscles underneath. "Well, she's got a good shoulder—should have a lot of reach. Deep girth, long underline…a bit light behind, though."

"You're right, she doesn't have a lot of speed."

I stepped back to take in the whole horse. The filly's eyes followed me, calm and brimming with intelligence. Overall, she was a plain horse, the colour of melting chocolate without a fleck of white anywhere on her. Still, there was something about her.

"She's got class," I said. And she did. Eve's Dream shone with that glow that all great horses carry about them. It went beyond the shine in her coat to shimmer in the air around her. It was there in the keen look in her eye, the proud carriage of her head.

Roy Laughlin thumped me on the back. "She does have that, doesn't she?"

"What's she done?"

"Not much. She started twice last year, ran middle of the pack both of her races. She's been slow to mature, and she needs the distance." He slipped the filly a mint from his pocket. She took it daintily, crunching it between her teeth.

"And this year?" We both ducked under the chain and stood outside the stall.

"She hasn't run. We've been training at home, up and down the hills. Brought her to town for a couple of works and that's all."

My heart sank. "Mr. Laughlin, your filly seems to be a nice horse, but—"

He held up his hand to cut me off. "If you've got any buts, don't come near our horse."

"Sir, I didn't mean—"

"Reid, with the right rider on her back this filly can win the Lady Perthshire. The question is: are you that rider?"

He must have gotten my back up with that last bit. Instead of running in the opposite direction from this backyard trainer with his barely tried racehorse, I found myself pleading for a chance to ride her.

"You're going to send her out on the track today, right?"

"I was going to take her with the pony," said Roy.

"Put me on her. Let's see how we get along."

"It's a good idea, Roy." Evie had joined us outside the stall. "I like this young fellow. He might just be the rider you've been looking for."

I gave Mrs. Laughlin my biggest smile to get on her good side. Since the horse was named after her, I figured Eve Laughlin must have some say in the matter of choosing a jockey.

"I don't know, Evie, I was hoping to get someone with more experience. No offence to you, Reid, but you look like kindergarten's not far behind you."

"Well, Mr. Laughlin, maybe experience is overrated," I heard myself saying. "Guts and determination can make up for a lack in that department, and I can tell you I've got double—no, triple helpings of both."

Evie Laughlin laughed. Roy squinted his eyes at me.

"You're hungry for it, aren't you, son? You want a *win*."

"I sure do, sir. And I want it to be a big win. A really big one."

Eve's Dream reached around and, letting out a long sigh, set her chin on my shoulder.

Which is how I found myself jogging the dark bay filly on the racetrack a short while later, Roy Laughlin hustling his fat grey Snowball to keep up beside us. Eve's Dream had an easy way of going, each stride covering a lot of ground with minimal effort. She didn't seem to be moving any faster than Snowball, but her longer step put her out in front until Roy and the fat grey dropped back and we were by ourselves. Dream continued her steady trotting. She felt happy to be out on the track, enjoying the movement of her well-tuned body. She was alert but relaxed underneath me, confident and amiable. I began to like her more and more.

After one circuit I clucked to her to lope. She shifted gears smoothly. There was none of Carmina's surging power, just a gentle swing and glide, her legs reaching out for more and more ground until she was galloping, snorting with pleasure in time with each stride. Roy's instructions were to blow her out for a quarter of a mile, so as we approached the eighth pole I set her down on the rail and asked for more.

Her body flattened as the red-and-white pole flashed past, her long legs swinging ahead to pull us through the air. I chirped, pumped my body, whistled and whooped. Her stride swung steadily on and on, longer and longer in that same relentless rhythm. We soared past the second red-and-white pole. I quit pushing, letting her gallop out on her own. She kept up that steady tempo in a long, flat gallop that felt like she could go forever.

She was a one-paced horse. Enough stamina to run all day and most of the night, but no speed. Not a lick.

I took care to pull her up gently, no jerking or jarring. After facing the infield for a few moments, I turned her all the way around and headed to the gap along the outside rail. Dream walked like an angel on a long rein, blowing softly, hardly taxed by the work. She held her head just high enough to show her good opinion of herself. Roy jogged up to meet us.

"She feels great," I said before he asked. "I like her. She tries real hard."

He nodded. "She's got heart. She'll give you everything she has. The rest is up to you."

I knew what he meant. Eve's Dream had some talent, but not a lot, not enough to overcome any rider errors. But she could win. If her jockey's timing and judgment were right on, she could win.

On the way back to Roy's barn we discussed Dream, her quirks—very few—and her strengths. She was good in the gate, although she broke slow, and would run her best race off the pace, coming on at the end to sweep past tiring front-runners. Talking about the filly's abilities, planning strategies for the race, I felt excitement beginning to rise up inside me again.

We were about to turn in to the shed row when I caught

sight of Mom, heading to the grooms' stand while Corky took Homer to the track. Gracie was with them, ridden by someone I didn't recognize. Something pulled Mom's gaze my way. She froze in her tracks, her eyes huge and dark circled. I kicked my feet free of the stirrups and jumped down. "I'll be right there," I told Roy.

Close up, Mom looked worse. Her eyelids were puffy and her face was pale. She looked at me without blinking, staring as if she hadn't seen me for a longer time than just one day.

"Mom. I'm sorry." I stopped. I didn't know what else to say.

"You're all right?"

"I'm good. I stayed at Ella's place," I said, hastily adding, "Her parents are there."

"I know. Ella just told me. And her mother phoned me last night."

I hadn't known that. "I'm sorry," I repeated. "I should have called you."

"You went somewhere safe. That's all that matters." She squinted her eyes, holding back tears.

I hugged her tight. "I just had to get away. Get my head together."

"Do you feel better now?"

"I do." I let go and smiled to prove it.

"That's good." She patted my shoulder, gave it a squeeze. "You know I love you, that I'm very proud of you."

"I know, Mom." I looked down, watching the toe of my boot trace circles in the dirt. "I love you, too." I heaved a sigh, getting ready to say what had to be said. "Mom, there's something I've got to tell you."

"I've got something to say, too."

"Go ahead."

Now it was her turn to sigh. "Reid, if you were trying to force my hand by running off like you did, well, I'm sorry, son, but it isn't going to work."

"What are you getting at?"

"I'm not changing riders on Carmina, Reid. Now I hope—no, I *expect* you to accept this like an adult, but if you can't, if you're going to run away because you can't have your own way—"

"Isn't that what you're trying to do—have *your* own way? You know I'm the best rider for Carmina. You know she'll try harder for me than anyone else, so why are you putting up Corky? Because you don't want me to be a jockey anymore, do you? Well, I've got news for you, this is my life, not yours. I've got my licence, and I've got a mount in the Lady Perthshire. Yes, Mom, that's right, I can get my own rides without any help from you."

"What are you talking about?"

"I'm on Eve's Dream. I just got the ride."

"Who on earth is Eve's Dream?"

"I'll tell you who she is—the horse that's going to beat all of you!" Satisfied with the shocked look on her face, I spun on my heel and stomped off.

"Reid! Come back here!"

Heads were turning, a few people staring right at me. I glared them down and they looked away, some even stepping back as if I'd pushed them. Mom called again.

I kept walking.

14.

Mr. Gervais—Doug—asked me to help him wash the family van the next afternoon when I was done at the track. I couldn't refuse, not after he and his wife had fed me and given me a place to stay, but I hadn't been sleeping well and was in need of a long nap. Up to a couple of days ago I'd been washing close to a dozen horses a day, which went a long way to satisfy any urge I had to play with water, but it seemed to be important to Doug to scrub and spray away the faint dust film clinging to his middle-aged vehicle.

I wondered why he didn't ask his son to give him a hand, not that it was any of my business, but I soon realized I had been selected for a reason.

"So, how's it going with your mother?" Doug asked, sloshing soapsuds over the hood.

"Not great," I admitted. "It seems like every time we try to talk to each other we just end up arguing."

"Hmm. Well, what about your father? Is it any easier to talk to him?"

Hadn't Ella told him? "He's not around."

"Not at all?"

"Nope."

His scrub brush slowed. "That's too bad. He's missing out on knowing a fine young man. So it's been just you and your mother all these years?"

"And Clement, my little brother. Corky, too, but he's closer to being a grandpa than a father because of his age."

"Are you close to this Corky?"

"Well, we're not getting along too good right now because he stole my mount in the Lady Perthshire right out from under me. Of course, I can't entirely blame him. My mother picked him to ride instead of me because she's been acting kind of weird since her accident, but he could have turned her down. But now I've got myself on another horse, and she's a good one. Every time I ride her, I like her better and better. In fact, I think that Corky Sinclair's in for one heck of a surprise, because Eve's Dream is going to win that race like a thief in the night."

"I see," said Doug Gervais, though it was plain he didn't. "Well, Reid, in a couple of weeks school will be starting up again."

"Don't remind me," I groaned.

"School's important, son, you know that."

"Yes, it is," I agreed obediently. *For some people*, I added silently.

"Think you'll have things worked out with your mother by then?"

"I don't know. I really don't."

"Well, Rita and I got to talking about your situation. We'd like to help you out. Reid, would you like to live here, maybe for a few months, maybe a whole year, until things get better for you at home?"

I gawked at him, caught off guard. "Wow, thank you. That's good of you and Mrs. Gervais."

"You're very welcome. You're a fine young man, Reid, and we think you have a lot of potential. It'd be a terrible pity to see you fall through the cracks. There'd be a few conditions, of course. We'd expect you to work hard at school and keep your marks up. We'd also want you to get a part-time job on weekends to make money toward your university education. I could talk to my brother, see if he has anything."

"You mean be a janitor?"

"Sometimes he has extra work cleaning windows, shampooing carpets, stuff like that."

"But then I couldn't be a jockey."

He set down his scrub brush, looked over at me and sighed. "Son, I'm not going to pretend to know much about horse racing, but from the little I've learned from you and Ella it seems like a tough game to make a decent living at. You're a smart boy, Reid, anybody can tell. How do you do in school? Top of your class?"

"No, but I make the honour roll most of the time."

"There you go. Go to university, Reid; earn yourself a degree that'll get you a good job, and you'll be set for life. Doesn't that make a lot of sense?"

"I guess so."

"This jockey business—where's it going to get you? If you're going to put all that time and hard work into doing something, choose a path that's going to pay off. You've got to be realistic. Why risk life and limb to earn a few bucks when there are easier ways to make a living?"

I had no answer to that, but he didn't seem to notice.

"When I left school, I went straight to work at the mill. All I could think of was making enough money to buy a pickup. I didn't even consider going and getting more education or learning a trade. There's not a day goes by that I don't kick myself in the you-know-what because I didn't get some kind of schooling. Keep your options open, Reid, that's all I can say—don't get yourself shut out."

I nodded to show I'd heard and dunked my sponge in the bucket. When it was heavy with soapy water I slapped it forcefully against the side of the van. It hit the metal with a thunk.

Doug shot me a sharp glance. "You okay there, Reid?"

"Yeah, I'm fine."

It was a lie. I felt edgy, like I was heading into a trap but couldn't sense just where it lay. I knew Mr. Gervais was a kind man, and the advice he'd given me was good—for most people.

To me it just sounded like a sentence to a long, slow death.

15.

I missed the horses. That night, after supper with the Gervais family, I went to see them. I just walked out the door without telling anyone where I was going. Not exactly polite, I knew, but I just didn't have any words to explain.

The shed row was empty, as I'd expected it to be. Short of my help, and still recovering from her injury, Mom had to be exhausted by this time of day. Most likely she was stretched out on a lounge chair outside the trailer, dozing off in the cool of the evening. I felt a sharp pinch of guilt at not packing my share of the load. We had to work things out, but how that was going to happen I had no idea.

Marty spotted me first and let out a nicker that was echoed down the line of stalls. I went from horse to horse, offering mints, rubbing my face against their bony, velvet-lined cheeks, even hugging the ones who'd tolerate it. I went to Carmina's stall last. She pinned her ears and swung around, hiding her head at the back of the stall.

"Hey there, pretty lady. Don't be like that. Come on, talk to me," I coaxed.

Her tail flicked in disdain. I propped myself against the door and waited. After a bit, when she decided I'd been ignored long enough, she turned back and greedily nipped a mint from my open palm.

I murmured endearments into her slender ears, scratched under her chin, smoothed down the thin white blaze bisecting her long face. When she stuck her tongue out for me to gently tug, I knew I was forgiven.

Something eased in my chest, letting me pull in a long, deep breath of air. I had the strange and beautiful feeling that being around horses always gave me, of my feet settling into the earth while my soul soared free. I couldn't have explained it to Mr. Gervais or anybody else in a million years. The best I could do was say I was alive. Really, truly alive.

And being up on the back of a horse? Well, that was living in a whole different dimension.

After Carmina had tired of my attention and returned to her hay, I headed over to the Laughlin shed row. Dusk was fading to black, blurring the edges of a pale horse ambling along the shed row packing a rider.

"Reid! You're back!" Clem slid down off Keno. I grabbed his skinny frame and gave him a quick hug before mussing his hair and tickling his ribs. I'd missed my little brother the last while.

He slapped my hands away, softly punched me in the gut and threw his arms around me again. "You're coming home now, right?"

"Not just yet."

"Why not? Because you're still mad at Mom? Why can't you two quit fighting?" He let go and stomped over to press his face into Keno's shoulder.

I grabbed his shoulder to turn him around, but he resisted. I let him be. "It's complicated."

"Now you sound just like Mom."

"Well, it is. Look, I can't deal with any of this stuff right now. I've got to keep focused on the races tomorrow, and that's easier for me to do when I'm staying at Ella's place."

"But we're your family! You should want to be with us." Tears filled his eyes.

"I do, but I just can't, not right now. I just…can't." Guilt churned in my stomach. I hadn't realized my brother would take my leaving so hard. "But I will be. I promise."

"Soon? You'll come home soon?"

"You bet. As soon as the races are over I'll come back."

He turned around, swiping his wrist under his nose. "You'd better."

"I got a mount in the big race," I told him.

"I heard. A no-hoper trained by some old farmer."

"Who told you that crap? You shouldn't listen to idiots, Clem. Eve's Dream is going to win that race."

"Against Carmina? You're kidding, right?"

I didn't need to hear that. I told myself Clem's opinion didn't matter, he was just a kid parroting what he'd heard other people saying, but his words shifted something inside. It was the first crack in my confidence, just a hairline, but I couldn't let it get any bigger. "Look, I've got to go now."

"Reid, no—"

"It's late, and you should be in bed. So should Keno; he needs his rest too. I'll see you tomorrow."

"And you'll come back, right?" Clem asked yet again.

"I'll come back."

"Make it a promise."

"I promise to come back tomorrow," I said. "Now get to bed, okay?" I hugged him and gave him a push to get him on his way. I was glad it was dark and he couldn't see my face.

As he and the old horse melted into the darkness, I felt another jab of guilt. I *would* come back to the trailer tomorrow, just like I'd said I would.

But I hadn't promised to stay.

After Clem left I changed my destination. I climbed the stairs of the empty grandstand until I was halfway up and sat down. I couldn't see it through the darkness, but I knew the finish wire was right across from me. I propped my elbows on my knees, rested my chin on my hands and let my mind drift. I was riding in the Lady Perthshire, tucked tight to my mount's withers, her mane slapping my face as she ran faster and faster, the wire shimmering before us while the rest of the field fell farther and farther behind.

"Reid?" called a man's voice behind me.

I jerked up, startled out of my waking dream. "Who is that?"

At the top of the stairs a shadow shifted. "It's Corky." The dark form moved closer. "Thought I'd find you here. You always did like to hide out in this place."

I said nothing, wanting to sink back into my fantasy. The good feeling was fading fast, stomped away with each echoing clomp of Corky's boots. I closed my eyes, trying to keep the details vivid. There was one very important element I needed to fill in—my horse's mane. Was it flame red or midnight black?

Corky settled down beside me. "I've been thinking about some things."

Abruptly the pictures in my head vanished. I sighed. "Like what?"

"Well, maybe I gave Tracy the wrong impression about how you managed while she was in the hospital."

"Are you saying you lied?"

"No, Reid, I did not lie. I was used to doing things a certain way and you did them another. Some of the stuff you did, well, I didn't see the sense of it, not at that time. So when your mom asked how you were coping, I gave her my opinions."

"You mean you told her I was royally screwing up," I said bitterly.

"Well, not quite—"

"Come on, Corky, tell the truth. You got Mom thinking I couldn't handle looking after the horses."

"Hey, it was a lot of responsibility for a sixteen-year-old kid."

"But you didn't stop there. You told her I wasn't riding them good."

"I never said that."

"No, you didn't come right out with it, but you sure did a lot of hinting. You got Mom scared, thinking I'm going to get hurt. And it wasn't just Mom; you did the same with Walt. And Leona Rogers. Why, Corky? Why would you do that to me? You've known me since I was little. You're the closest person I've ever had to a father. I looked up to you. I wanted to be just like you."

"No, you don't. You don't want to be that," he said thickly. "You want to set your sights a lot higher than that."

"You did this to get the ride on Carmina, didn't you?"

He heaved a long sigh. "Reid, that's why I'm here. You still want to ride the filly tomorrow, she's yours. Just say the word."

"You're giving up the ride on Carmina?"

"I'm turning it over to you. You and Clem and your mom—you're important to me. You're family. If giving you the ride in this race will fix things up between all of us, well, then, that's what I've got to do. Hell, I'd give you my rides in a dozen races just to put things back to the way they were."

"But it's an important race. You're getting old, Corky, for a jockey. This could be your last chance to win a big race."

"I know that."

"You sure changed your mind all of a sudden."

"Yeah, well, I figure I've got to mend some fences before they fall apart."

"So how would you make this happen?"

"Don't worry about that. I'm a little guy who's spent most of my life persuading hot-headed animals ten times my size to do what I want them to—people are easy to handle." He paused. "So you want to switch?"

"I...I don't know."

"What do you mean? What's going on with you, Reid? I'm giving you the biggest break of your life."

"I know, I know!"

"Let me tell you, a horse like Carmina doesn't come along just every day. She's once in a lifetime. You might never get to ride a horse like her ever again. Good Lord, if someone had handed me this chance on a silver platter when I was your age, I'd have been all over it."

Everything he said made sense; I'd thought it myself a hundred times. I worked my jaw, getting ready to say yes.

The word wouldn't come out.

The picture flashed into my mind, bright and clear. The finish wire ahead, a grandstand alongside and a long neck stretched out under me, ears flat to the skull, mane blowing in my face.

"So what's it going to be, Reid? What horse are you going to ride?"

I took in a long breath, then gave him my answer.

16.

The moment I strode into the walking ring with the other jockeys late the next afternoon, I knew I'd done the right thing. Watching my filly prance around the ring with the other entries in the Lady Perthshire, I was filled with a calm certainty.

Up until then I hadn't been sure. As soon as I'd made my choice, I started questioning it. So did almost everyone else—Corky, Clem, even Ella. I woke up twice in the night wondering if I'd imagined the sudden pulse in my guts that had told me what to say to Corky.

The only person who didn't second-guess my choice was my mother. And Roy and Evie Laughlin, of course.

Once the Laughlins had picked me as their jockey, their faith in me was absolute. I'd done everything I could to show I deserved it riding my two earlier mounts. I'd hustled Country Magic up to a second-place finish and then had come from off the pace with Justabayboy to place third by two lengths. Good rides, both of them, but now it was time to do even better.

I shook Evie's hand, then Roy's, and was introduced to their grown-up children and grandkids. Then my trainer gave me his instructions:

"Ride her like she's yours, son, and the feed tub's empty."

I was still laughing when a hand settled on my arm. I turned to see who it was. Mom took hold of my hand and shook it.

"Good luck, Reid. You made a good choice." Her smile was genuine. Her eyes held mine, steady and confident.

"Thanks, Mom."

"Your filly has some talent. I won on her mother, you know. At this track."

I smiled. I hadn't known, but I wasn't surprised.

"Riders up!"

Mom squeezed my hand again before hurrying away to leg her jockey up.

"Five!" called the paddock judge.

I scuttled up alongside Dream and bent my left leg out behind me. Roy grabbed it and tossed me high onto her back. I dangled my feet down her sides while I knotted my reins. The filly danced a few steps on her tiptoes.

"You're feeling good today, aren't you, my girl?" I reached forward and patted Dream's neck, relieved to find the soft, glossy hair under my palm completely dry.

The black filly just ahead of us flung her head wildly and skittered sideways, revealing a neck darkened with sweat. She was close to leaving her race right here in the paddock, her excitement consuming precious reserves of energy that she would need for the long run ahead. In contrast, Dream felt relaxed but alert underneath me.

I grinned over at my trainer and owners and gave them a thumbs-up.

The others believed I'd picked Dream because I didn't want to disappoint Roy and Evie. I let them think that, but the truth was I'd decided to ride her because I knew she could win.

If she got the right race. I was going to do my best to make sure she did.

"You're a star, Dream horse," I muttered. Her long ears twitched back to listen. "A superstar."

She snorted, throwing her head and rolling her eyes back to look at me. I wondered how much she understood.

Ahead of us, Carmina was bounding around the walking ring in giant frog leaps, Corky bouncing on her back like a bronc rider. Mom had herself and another handler on her, one on each side, instead of just the usual one on the left. Both were leaning hard against the lead shanks, trying to keep the big filly from launching herself and her rider into outer space. At that moment I didn't envy Corky, not at all.

"Reid! Reid, over here!" Ella and Clem shouted to me from outside the walking ring. I was surprised to see all the rest of the Gervais family with them, smiling and cheering. I grinned and tapped my whip handle on my hat brim to show I'd seen them.

Then we were being led out onto the track for the post parade, and it was time to focus.

The slim chocolate-brown neck arched in front of me. Dream pranced past the grandstand, playing to the crowd. We had the five post so we were right in the middle of the parade. The horses in front began to trot, warming up. I knew Dream had shifted gaits because her rhythm had changed, her peculiar gliding stride barely jolting me in the saddle.

We were surrounded by a bubble, the filly and I. All the noise of the outside world faded away until there was only the steady drumbeat of hooves. My heart beat out the same rhythm—one, two, one, two. The filly and I melded into a single organism, faster and more powerful than the sum of our two separate parts.

I had never felt this way before, not on any horse.

And then the starter called us to the gate. The protective bubble dissolved. Sound burst out all around us—voices calling, gates slamming shut, the distant crackle of the announcer. I realized my limbs were shaking, adrenalin rushing unchecked through my blood. Dream jigged, fussing at the bit, her tail lashing against her quarters. I forced air through my nose into my lungs, taking control of my body again.

A member of the gate crew was at the filly's head, leading her into the starting stall. He clambered up onto the pontoon. Behind us the gate rattled shut.

Dream shifted uneasily in the narrow confines. I murmured reassurance and pulled down my goggles.

Out of the corner of my eye I saw the last stalls filling with horses. Joel Mack's good grey filly, Ice Storm, was three stalls over. I set my feet forward and took up my reins. Dream's long ears were turned forward, framing my view of the broad ribbon of sand stretching in front of us. She set her chin in the V of the front gate.

The last stall gate clanged. Dream and I were ready, poised and alert.

The filly tensed, ever so slightly, as the tiny current of electricity passed through the front gates just before they opened. My muscles responded, the barrier sprang open and we burst out onto the track.

We were in the clear, empty space all around us. I could tell by the distance of the noise behind us—ringing bells and shouting and pounding hooves—that we had two jumps, maybe even more, on the rest of the field. Joyous excitement swept through me. In an instant I threw aside my game plan to take advantage of this unexpected bonus. I urged Dream on, angling across the track for the rail, opening up on the field.

We gained the rail. Dream was into her full stride, legs swinging out and pulling the ground past in a metronome rhythm. I quit pushing and let her settle. The thunder of hooves crescendoed behind us as the field chased us down. My filly reached out, ready to run away from the other horses again, but I held her back.

Moments later we were swamped by horses. They were alongside, passing us, dropping down inside onto the rail to take over our lead. We dropped back to fifth place, a trio forming a solid wall of horseflesh in front of us while another horse tucked in on our right side. Going into the first turn, Dream and I were completely blocked in. We were saving ground running on the rail, but we had no place to go.

Take it easy, I cautioned myself, *this is a long race. There's a lot of running ahead.*

My filly was settled, running easily beneath me. In front, the massive hindquarters of the horse one off the rail were coming closer. I recognized Carmina and knew Corky was trying to steady her back to save some of her speed for the end of the race. Carmina veered back and forth, resisting her rider's hold. The jockey on her outside screeched out a warning as she brushed up against his mount.

Corky let the filly go. It was the right decision. Carmina wasn't going to tolerate being held back and would waste energy fighting him.

Dream's ears pricked as those powerful quarters pulled away. My filly wanted to go too.

"No, sweetheart, not yet," I crooned to her. "Be patient, that's my girl."

The chocolate-brown ears twitched back to listen to my voice. Dream relaxed back into her steady, sweeping stride.

In front of us, Carmina was pulling farther and farther ahead. Halfway down the backstretch she had opened up seven lengths or more on the rest of the field. Corky couldn't hold the filly back, couldn't save some of her fantastic speed for the end of the race, so he was doing the only thing he could—letting the filly run so far away from the other horses that no one could catch her before the finish line.

It was a bold move and a risky one. Every filly in this race was a talented runner. If Carmina didn't put in enough distance, if she tired too soon and her speed dropped off, the entire field could catch her and pass on by.

With her red flame of a tail flying away down the track, it seemed that was never going to happen. Carmina was going to run away with the race.

The rider outside me sent his horse after the big red filly. More horses came up beside Dream. We entered the second turn in drill-team formation, a solid pack of horses running stride for stride. Over the constant thunder of hooves, riders shrieked to their mounts, cajoling, urging them on after Carmina.

Too soon, I told myself. *It's way too soon.*

But was it? I felt my own nerve falter, began to wonder if I'd made a mistake. Had I laid too far off the pace for too long?

Had I made the classic rookie mistake of riding a plan and not the race?

A fierce determination rose up in me, more powerful than anything I'd ever felt before. I had to win this race. *Had* to. I would be nobody's pet apprentice, no one's little boy any longer. My talents, my abilities, my skills would be all my own. All the world would see me for who I was, a jockey in my own right.

My blood was on fire. My head was cool. I was going to make this happen. I let my mount go with the other horses.

Dream was running like a veteran, hugging the rail for the shortest trip through the turn.

Even so, we still had nowhere to run. A ragged line of horses was strung across the track in front of us to form a blockade anchored at the front by Carmina, still one over from the rail. The horse on the rail was coming back to us, tiring from the furious pace. Any moment now I was going to have to check Dream, pull her back to avoid clipping heels with the other horse. We were hemmed in, trapped by the horses in front and the horse on our outside.

And then it finally happened. Coming out of the turn Carmina switched leads, her right leg leading, and shifted over toward the middle of the track.

Like she always did.

A horse burst out of the blockade, chasing after Carmina. All around us horses and their jockeys were changing position, trying to find running room. Without turning my head, I sensed the horse beside us move over, just a little, but it was enough. A gap appeared next to the horse on the rail. Not much of an opening, but wide enough for a slim horse like Dream to go through.

I sent her toward it.

This was the moment I'd been waiting for—but I hadn't reckoned on being so far behind Carmina when it came. We had to take that opening before another horse did.

Dream's relentless swinging stride carried us up a length, then two. This final stretch of track leading to the finish wire was a long one; lots of time yet for Dream to move up on the leaders. Excitement fizzed through my veins, feeding new energy to my tiring muscles. I tucked in tight to my filly's withers and called out encouragement.

Dream bore down another length. Carmina loomed before us. Corky was nearly dancing in the saddle, riding hard to keep the filly together and focused.

Out of the corner of my right eye I caught a flash of silver. Ice Storm came up close on Carmina's outside and stalled there. Both horses were weary, wobbling in their paths. They split apart and then came together again, bumping shoulders.

The impact knocked Corky's foot out of his stirrup. He lurched over Carmina's shoulder, heaved himself up to sprawl on her neck. His left hip began to slide off the tiny saddle.

Dream was two strides back. I shouted to her and she reached out, stretching her stride even further.

One stride away. Corky was tipping over the filly's side into our path. I felt Dream's surprise. She faltered, started to shift over. "Come on, girl, get up there."

She drew alongside Carmina. I reached over and braced my hand against Corky's shoulder. He pushed himself back on top of his horse. I caught a glimpse of his eyes, round as a goldfish's behind his goggles.

Ice Storm had passed us both and was running to the wire.

Beneath me, Dream felt fresh and eager, her strides still coming long and straight and true. I let her go after the grey filly, knowing we needed a miracle to catch that silver tail streaking away in front of us.

I chirped and clucked to my brave filly. I called and kissed and hollered as if we were close to coming up on the filly far ahead, as if we had a chance of passing her.

And then, somehow, Dream was closing the gap. Her legs reached out and closed with greater speed, pulling us closer and closer to the tiring Ice Storm until we were right alongside. I was screaming for real, my gutsy, beautiful Dream giving everything she had to keep up with the other horse.

The roar of the grandstand crowd hit us like a tidal wave. The finish line was just ahead. Only a few strides away. Neck to neck, matching strides, the two gallant fillies ran toward it.

My knee was just in front of the other rider's. Three strides to the wire, then two, and one.

Eve's Dream reached out, extending every limb as far as it would go, stretching her long neck to put her nose out in front as we swept under the wire.

17.

We went halfway down the backstretch again before I could pull Dream up.

My throat was taut and dry in a way that had nothing to do with being short of air. Something wet leaked from my eyes and dribbled down my cheeks. There was a feeling rising up in me that threatened to crack through my ribs and burst my chest right open. I wanted to throw back my head and roar at the heavens.

We'd done it—*we* had—this magnificent plain brown filly and I. Almost no one had believed we could win, but win we did—through determination, skill and heart.

We'd come first under the wire.

Watching my tears fall in shiny blobs on Dream's black mane, I knew nothing was ever going to be the same again.

The outrider caught up with us, and we turned around. Dream was blowing hard, but she held her head high, her long, thin ears alert. When we came around the turn she halted, listening to the roaring, stomping grandstand. She heaved a great sigh.

"Come on, Dream, they're waiting for you at the winner's circle."

She resumed walking, her head held high.

"The results aren't official yet," warned the outrider. "It was a photo finish, and there's a steward's inquiry."

I nodded, unconcerned.

"That was some great riding, kid. Catching Corky Sinclair like that—you could get work as a stunt rider in the movies."

Then we were before the grandstand, the cheering of the crowd rolling over us in waves. Roy Laughlin took his filly by the bridle, blinking away tears.

"Thank you, son, thank you, thank you," he said over and over, stroking Dream's neck as he led us around in small circles.

That started the water running in my eyes again.

Everyone was calling my name, throwing congratulations at me from all sides. I didn't know which way to look, what direction to turn. I raised my hand and saluted them all.

Scanning the heads below me, I spotted my mother unsaddling a stamping, fussing Carmina. She pulled off the tack and turned, catching my eye. A huge grin covered her face as she pumped a fist in the air.

I clenched my hand and held it up, mirroring her.

Then Mom did something I didn't quite understand. Hand still above her head, she opened it, palm facing me, and slowly waved. Her smile remained steadfast, but even at a distance I saw her swallow hard.

And then the stewards declared the results official.

Swiping his sleeve over his eyes, Roy led us to the winner's circle. Evie Laughlin and a truckload of relatives, friends and hangers-on gathered round for the presentation and photo. "Come on, you two," she called, beckoning, and Clem and Ella scurried over to squeeze into the group. "Anyone missing?"

"Mom!" I called, but she was nearly off the track, following her horse back to the barn.

And that's what my first win photo shows—a crowd of people surrounding a lean, chocolate-brown filly, who is gazing into the distance with the look of eagles. The jockey on her back with the crooked smile is looking past the camera too, staring at something beyond the lens.

I can recall just what was going through my head the very moment the photographer took that picture. I was remembering those final strides as Dream and I struggled against all odds to be first across the finish line.

I had looked up at the thin wire strung across the race-track. High in the air, backed by the blue sky and catching the sun, it gleamed like a thread of gold.

"It's him!"

The first bucket of water sloshed over me. I scrambled back, but someone was blocking the jocks' room door. Then the water was coming from all around me, bucketful after bucketful. All I could do was grin and bear it.

The riders formed a circle. Corky stood before me, holding a bucket. "Congratulations on winning your first race, kid. You did good." With great ceremony he lifted the bucket and poured a cascade of water over me amid cheers and catcalls. He hugged me hard, then held me at arm's length. "Thank you, Reid. I owe you."

He winked and slapped me on the shoulder.

I blinked hard, getting all that water out of my eyes.

Grabbing a towel, I dried my face. Then I stripped off my wet silks and had another shower, a warm one.

I dried off and dressed in an oddly deserted jocks' room. Gathering up my gear, I went outside.

The first muffled giggle should have warned me. I gasped as another bucket of cold water hit me. Clem pranced around, laughing hysterically and waving the empty bucket.

Then Ella raced around the corner of the building and dumped her bucket over me. Shaking water out of my hair and eyes, I caught hold of her wrist and pulled her close. I could have stared forever into those caramel-brown eyes, basking in the warmth and admiration shining out from them, but Ella reached out and pulled my lips to hers.

I felt myself floating, head over heels and back again. I was halfway to heaven when she pulled back with a tiny frown.

"What? Is something wrong?" I croaked.

She twisted her head to look over her shoulder. "What's that noise?"

It was Clem pretending to puke. Now that he'd gotten our attention, he skipped around like a demented monkey. "Reid's got a girlfriend! Reid's got a girlfriend!"

I traced my fingers over Ella's cheek. "Have I?"

She smiled and nodded.

Now Clem was making loud kissy sounds. Ella cocked an eyebrow. "He's being pretty obnoxious, don't you think?"

"He sure is."

"Let's get him!"

Together we turned and rushed Clem. He squirmed loose and ran off, shrieking at the top of his lungs. Laughing,

Ella and I chased him all the way to the campground.

Every single person in the campground and more besides were gathered at our trailer. "Hey there, young fellow, what's going on?" asked Corky as Clem threw himself at him.

"Save me! Don't let Reid get me!" Clem giggled wildly as Corky hoisted him upside down and shook him up and down.

Evie Laughlin hugged me. "Oh my goodness, you're soaking wet!"

I glanced down at my dripping clothes. "Sorry about that. I'll get changed."

She took my hand in both of hers and gently squeezed. "Reid, winning that race: it means so much to us. We can't thank you enough. You are an amazing young man, do you know that?"

"You're very welcome, Mrs. Laughlin, but I should be thanking you for letting me ride your filly. She's got class, that girl." I turned to Roy, standing next to his wife with his arm around her waist. "When do you plan on running her next? I'd sure like to have the ride on her again."

The Laughlins looked at each other. "Well, that's the thing, son," said Roy, carefully studying the toe of his boot. "Racing's a tough business, you know. We're going to end on a high note, take the filly home to the farm, give her some retraining so our granddaughter can ride her. Maybe we'll get a few foals out of her, too."

"So you're not going to run her anymore?" I couldn't hide my disappointment.

"No, Reid, we're sorry, but Dream's run her last race."

Ella squeezed my hand, sharing my disappointment.

"Now, don't you worry, young man, you've got a bright future ahead of you," Roy went on. "The ride you gave our filly today made a lot of folks sit up and take notice."

"Everyone's talking about how you saved Corky Sinclair. I didn't see it happen, but they're all calling you a hero!" said Evie.

I thanked them again, then slipped inside the trailer to get into dry clothes. I rubbed my hair with a towel and combed it flat. Setting my hands on the sink I studied myself in the mirror. I didn't look any different. I hadn't changed at all, but already people were seeing me differently.

"This is only the beginning," I said to my reflection. I watched my mouth stretch up in a big smile. I was still grinning when I went back outside.

More people came over to congratulate me on my first win. Tables were pushed together and loaded with food; barbecues were sending off delicious smells. Evie Laughlin pushed a paper plate heaped with salads and barbecued chicken at me. My belly rumbled loud enough for everyone to hear.

"Now, you eat that up, every last bit," said Evie sternly.

I looked around for a place to park and saw my mother's empty chair. I scanned the crowd for a blonde head and couldn't find her. I snagged Clem by the collar of his shirt.

"Where's Mom?"

He shrugged. "She was here a few minutes ago. With Mrs. Rogers and Walt and some other guys."

Corky bumped my shoulder. "Hey, Reid, come with me. There are some guys who want to meet you."

"I've got my supper here." I held up my full plate.

He took it out of my hands and passed it to Ella. "They're over at the barn."

Another party had sprung up in our shed row. Walt and two men in expensive weekend clothes were beside Carmina's stall, grinning and patting each other on the back. Leona Rogers' hands fluttered about as she spoke to Mom, who was tying a piece of bale twine in elaborate knots.

"Here he is," announced Corky. Everyone turned to look at me. "Reid, this is Bill Lewis and Jasper Goodwell."

"The trainer?" I asked, shaking Mr. Goodwell's hand.

He nodded. "Pleased to meet you, Reid. Corky's been telling us a lot about you. We go back a long way, you know.

Used to ride together."

"A long time ago. And about forty pounds, eh?" Corky chuckled and jabbed Jasper Goodwell in the belly with his finger.

Bill Lewis coughed and looked at his watch. "We need to leave soon, Jasper, to make our flight."

"Right, down to business."

I moved over to Carmina's door. The filly was at the back of her stall, one hip slouched, her head hanging.

"Hey, pretty lady, how's it going?"

She snaked her head at me, flat-eared.

"Come on, don't be like that. I know, I know, you're upset about losing, but you can be friendly, yes, you can, that's my girl." She put her head over the stall guard and let me scratch her withers. "That feels good, doesn't it?"

"See, what did I tell you? He can get this filly to do anything!" said Corky.

The two strangers looked at me and then each other. Bill Lewis shrugged and nodded.

"Reid, how would you like to ride for us?" asked Jasper.

"What? You mean here?"

Bill Lewis laughed out loud. Jasper shook his head. "No, no, back east. Most of our horses are at Woodbine in Toronto, and of course we go south for the winter."

I narrowed my eyes, shot Corky a suspicious glance.

"Are you serious? Is this some kind of joke?"

"No, Reid, it's not," said Mom. "Mr. Lewis has just bought Carmina."

"What? Who's going to train her?"

"Jasper trains all my horses," said Bill Lewis.

"So she's leaving." A bitter taste filled my mouth. I glared at Walt and Mrs. Rogers. "This isn't right. You've got no business doing this to us. We've worked so hard at getting this filly turned around, and the moment she starts doing good you sell her out from under us."

Leona pressed her hands to her cheeks. Walt stepped in front of her. "That's enough from you."

Mom's hands settled on my shoulders. "Reid, it's okay."

"No, it's not! Carmina's a talented filly. She's going places."

"I know she is, son. Listen," she said firmly, giving me a shake. "*I* told Leona to sell her."

"You did? But…why?"

"I told you before, it's time to make some changes. Do something different."

I stared at her, trying to understand what she could possibly want to change. "Mom, a horse like Carmina doesn't come along every day. You could wait the rest of your life to get another filly as good as she is to train."

"I know." She didn't seem at all upset.

Finally I got it. I recalled our talk about going to live on Leona Rogers' farm as the caretaker. This time I remembered something else: the delight in my mother's voice as she described the new mobile home with the skylights, the river, the two dogs. That was why she wasn't disappointed about losing Carmina to another trainer. It was the first step in a new direction for her life.

Somewhere along the way our dreams had parted company.

"Reid, you haven't answered Jasper," said Corky.

Mom's hands fell away. I turned back to the two men. Mr. Lewis looked at his watch again.

"The thing is, we need someone right away. One of our exercise riders is out for a couple of months," said Jasper. He rubbed at his chin and sighed. "I suppose I can give you a day or two to think it over, if that's what you need."

And then I understood. Life is just like a horse race: you go in with a plan, but you have to ride the race as it happens, ready to run through the openings that come your way.

"I'll do it," I said to Jasper Goodwell. "I'll ride for you."

18.

A sharp April breeze blew across the paddock as I came out of the jocks' room. I pulled up the collar of my silks against the rain needling the back of my neck.

My owner was waiting for me in the walking ring with a small group of people. They let out a ragged cheer at the sight of me.

I shook hands with Jasper and Mr. Lewis. I moved along the line to Mom, Clem and Corky, giving them all big hugs. It was the first time I'd seen my family since I'd left at the end of summer the year before. We'd talked or texted nearly every day, but seeing them in person made me realize how much I'd missed them all.

"You made it! I was starting to wonder if you were going to miss the race."

"The plane was late," said Corky. "I was ready to jump out and run all the way across the country. No way was I going to miss your first race at Woodbine."

"Oh, Reid." Mom clasped my hands tightly. "It's so good to see you. How is it at the Goodwells? Are you happy there?"

I lived with Jasper and Irene Goodwell. "I am, Mom. The Goodwells are really nice. Irene's like...like an aunt to me. But I told you all this already."

"I needed to hear it again. So how's your schooling going?" Mom let go of me and stepped back. She wore a dress and high heels and had her hair in a new style, up on top of her head. She looked rested and relaxed and...well, happy.

"Great! I'm just about done. Only five more courses to go and I'm finished." I was taking classes online, having promised Mom I'd get my Grade Twelve. I couldn't wait to be done. With so much happening in my life, getting through those stupid courses was a real chore.

Mom studied my face. "You look different."

"It's the tan. We haven't been back from Florida very long."

"So you liked it down south, eh?" said Corky.

"It was fantastic! Everything was great—the weather, the people and the horses. Corky, I've never been on so many good horses in my life. I wish I could have ridden more of them in the afternoon."

"Yeah, well, that's going to happen. You rode good in those three races down there, 'specially the last one. People will notice."

"Sorry I didn't make it home for Christmas," I said, mostly to my mother. "It just would have been too rushed for me to get back in time for Boxing Day." I'd ridden in my second race the day after Christmas.

"We missed you, Reid, but we understand," she said. "You have to take every ride you get offered when you're starting out."

Clem fussed with the tie wrapped around his scrawny neck.

"Hey, look at you, dude." I mussed his hair. "Nice clothes."

"Mom made me wear them. This tie's choking me!"

"So you like living on the farm, huh?"

He nodded. "My friends Jason and David come over all the time because we've got the best fishing on the river. They want to meet you, next time you come home."

Mom and Clem had moved onto Leona Rogers'—make that Fletcher's—farm while the new Mr. and Mrs. Fletcher travelled around North America in the motorhome they'd bought after selling Carmina. Mom had passed the outside horses on to other trainers and was retraining Singalong Susie, Bright Grace, Goingmyway, Marty and Homer so they could go on to new careers as jumpers and polo ponies. Clem had taken up fly-fishing on the river that ran through the place. Keno was pretty much retired to pasture except for when Clem jumped on him bareback with his fly rod and rode him down to the river.

It was a pretty quiet life after the track, but Mom's old friends came visiting, along with a new one, a Dr. Kevin Matthews—who happened to be an avid fly-fisher, Clem told me with approval. I was glad, for both of them.

I'd noticed right away there was no fourth member of my fan club. "Ella?"

"She couldn't make it, Reid," said Mom.

"Couldn't? Or wouldn't?" I'd been so busy, it had taken me nearly a month to realize Ella's texts had dwindled from daily to just a few in a week. "There's someone else, isn't there?"

Mom shrugged and sighed. "I think so. I've got a letter from her to give you."

Ella had stayed in touch with Mom, going to the farm some weekends to help out when she could get a ride.

"Later. After the race."

"Riders up!"

My trainer boosted me onto my horse, a workmanlike four-year-old using this race as a conditioner for an upcoming stakes. My debut race at Woodbine had been carefully chosen.

I gathered my reins and grinned down at my family.

"Good luck!" they chorused.

I nodded my thanks. Just as my horse stepped onto the track, the sun burst out of the clouds. I felt its warmth full on my face. All around me the air seemed to be sparkling.

We paraded past the stands. My mount was up on his toes, bright and eager and ready to run.

Somehow he reminded me of Ella. His mane was even the same colour as her hair.

I felt a pang of loss. I wasn't surprised she was moving on. I'd left an opening and someone else had gone right through it.

Could it have been any other way?

We approached the starting gate. Ella and the rest of the world vanished. As we circled, waiting to be loaded, the colours of the riders' silks gleamed, the clattering of the metal gates took on musical tones.

My horse went in. I pulled down my goggles, set my feet, took up my reins. My vision telescoped to a broad strip of green turf rolling away in front of me.

I could feel my heart rate quicken, pounding rich red blood through my veins with the steady beat of a metronome.

I felt completely, incredibly *alive*.

"Ready for this, kid?" asked the header, crouched beside my horse's head on the pontoon.

"I am. I've been ready for years."

The final horse loaded. For a brief moment, time hung suspended around us.

The gates flung open and we burst out, a wave of horses and riders charging onto the grass.

Absolute joy filled every cell of my body. I shouted with delight, the sound mingling with the whistling and clucking and catcalls around us.

Then I settled down to ride, giving it everything I had to be first under the wire.

Julie White has spent a lifetime riding and working with horses. She and her husband, a former jockey, live on a horse farm in Armstrong, British Columbia, where they raise and train Thoroughbreds for racing and jumping. An avid reader, Julie works part-time in a tiny library in the country that some of her customers travel to on horseback.

More pony adventures from author Julie White

The Secret Pony

Kirsty's got a secret—a big, four-legged secret

When they moved out to the country after the divorce, Mom promised Kirsty a pony of her own. Unfortunately, money is tighter than they expected. Then Lancelot practically drops in Kirsty's lap, and she empties her money box to buy him. He's skinny and starved and only half trained. But he's hers. The problem is, she can't seem to find the words to tell her mother that the pony she'll be riding is her own.

☆ *Our Choice Award*   ☆ *Chocolate Lily Award*

High Fences

Robin is a pony in a million. He'll do anything Faye asks him to do, and Faye loves him with all her heart.

When Faye's grandmother Lucy starts talking about selling the farm, Faye does the unthinkable. She agrees to sell Robin.

It's galling that Robin's new owner is Nicole, a pampered, pretty rider with no notion of how to handle him. Then a wonderful opportunity arrives, and Faye has to face the truth. Maybe there's a time when winning means losing the best partner you've ever had.

Riding Through Fire

It's been hot and dry for months, and it's not just the weather that's getting to Kirsty. She's feeling a bit left out, with her best friend Faye enjoying the show-jumping world as a professional rider. So, when Lucy asks, Kirsty agrees to help with a mountain cattle drive. She's nervous, but at least it's not the usual chores.

It's too bad that Kirsty gets stuck with Jesse, a teenager with a big attitude problem. They get lost—and then they smell fire. Suddenly, this is no usual round-up…and Kirsty will learn, more than she ever expected, that Lancelot is no usual pony.